CW01508107

THREE'S COMPANY

N.R. WALKER

BLURB

When he started looking for someone to help heal his broken heart, Wilson Curtis never dreamed he'd find two someones.

After Wilson Curtis was publicly outed, his restaurant business left in tatters, and dumped by his closeted boyfriend, he goes to Key West alone. There he meets Simon Stanford and Adam Preston. Fascinated by this couple, he is soon invited into their bed for some holiday fun.

But once isn't enough, and the offer is extended for the remainder of his stay. As they get to know each other, in and out of the bedroom, sparks fly, and ten days is all it takes to change their lives.

When it comes time for Wil to leave, with tensions closing in and time running out, tempers flare and emotions fray. Beneath the physical attraction and the foolish misunderstandings is the realization these three men aren't ready to say goodbye.

Wil soon learns that love isn't always conventional, and the only thing better than giving your heart to one man, is giving it to two.

DEDICATION

For an idea that started out as some 'cabana boys' and morphed into something else entirely, Brenda Gibson, this one's for you.

COPYRIGHT

Cover Artist: Reese Dante
Editor: Labyrinth Bound Edits
Publisher: BlueHeart Press
Three's Company © 2012 N.R. Walker
Third Edition 2018

All Rights Reserved:

This literary work may not be reproduced or transmitted in any form or by any means, including electronic or photographic reproduction, in whole or in part, without express written permission.
This is a work of fiction, and any resemblance to persons, living or dead, or business establishments, events or locales is coincidental, except in the case of brief quotations embodied in critical articles and reviews.
The Licensed Art Material is being used for illustrative purposes only.

Warning

Intended for an 18+ audience only. This book contains material that maybe offensive to some and is intended for a mature, adult audience. It contains graphic language, explicit sexual content, and adult situations.

Trademarks

All trademarks are the property of their respective owners.

N.R. WALKER

Three's
COMPANY

PROLOGUE

SIMON

ADAM WAS GETTING RESTLESS. Every now and again, he'd get antsy, and now was one of those times. We'd been together long enough that I knew the signs. He found it hard to keep still on any given day, but this was different. He'd fidget, he'd swim for longer in the mornings, and he'd beg for us to hit the town after work.

He'd also want to drink and dance, which was something he didn't want to do often. It would burn off that agitated energy, buzzing just under his skin.

He'd also want to find someone else to fuck.

We'd been together for almost three years and were solely exclusive, faithful, committed. Except for our need, every so often, to bring another man into our bed. It was purely a physical thing. It was the best of both worlds—fun, sexy, exciting, and it allowed us to be adventurous together. Then when the other guy was gone, we'd go back to our status quo of being a committed, monogamous couple.

We didn't view it as cheating because it wasn't. We did it together, both of us willingly. We discussed it openly, and both of us had to agree to do it. Both of us had to be there, or it didn't happen, and rarely did it happen with the same guy more than once.

There were no emotions involved. It was just pure lust, a sexual itch that needed scratching a few times a year.

"You know what you need?" I said, kissing the back of his neck. I'd closed up the hotel, and Adam was cleaning up his bar. I stood behind him and wrapped my arms around him.

"What's that?"

"We need to go find some lucky guy and make his holiday-threesome dreams come true."

Adam turned his head a little and leaned back into me. "Is that right?"

"If you want to, that is."

"Do you want to?"

I snorted quietly and nuzzled my nose into the back of his head. "Do you really have to ask?"

Adam turned and settled his hands on my hips, pulling us together. "Yes, I do."

I cupped his face with both my hands and softly kissed his lips. "I want us to go find someone to bring back here or take into the backroom of the nightclub, or whatever. We could take it turns fucking him, or you could fuck him and I could sandwich you in the middle. You'd be buried in his ass and I'd be buried in you."

He shivered and gooseflesh crept over his skin. "Sy," he said gruffly. "You're so good to me."

I kissed him, harder this time. "And you're so good to me."

He seemed to bask in the adoration, letting my love for him expand in his chest.

"So, tonight? Or tomorrow night?"

"No time like the present."

The bar was packed. It was tourist season in the Keys, and there was a dance floor of swaying and sweaty men to choose from. Adam and I danced for a while, scouting for anyone who we might want to join us in a little ménage.

It wasn't like anyone wasn't interested. We'd involved a few local guys in our time together who were more than keen for a second time, but we preferred the non-complicated. One-night stands, never to be seen again, emotionless. I suggested a few guys with no more than a nod in their direction, but after Adam checked them out, he gave a subtle shake of his head.

None of them were right.

I happened to agree with him. Sure, they were hot enough and would probably have served their purpose well. But it was something I couldn't put my finger on. To put it bluntly, like I'd said before, none of them were right. Admittedly, we'd never been all too fussy about who we picked up. If there was an attraction, it was on.

So we left it for that night. If it wasn't going to happen, it just wasn't going to happen.

But then the next weekend, we tried again. We scouted the bar, checking out the possibilities, but none of them were... right.

Maybe we were bored with the idea. Clearly we now had standards, and they were not being met. Or maybe, just maybe, we were looking for something more.

I was so happy with Adam. We were complete, just the way we were. We just liked to play with a third guy every now and again, and that in no way reflected what we were as a couple. We were solid. Unbreakable.

After the next week, a still-restless Adam didn't want to hit the bars again. I assumed he didn't want to be disappointed. I didn't blame him.

"We'll find someone when the time is right," I reassured him.

He nodded and gave me his best smile. "Yeah, it's no big deal," he said, though he'd always been a crappy liar.

And that itch, the itch only a third person could reach, remained unscratched.

For the next week, I didn't give it much thought. Adam seemed happy enough, and I had some appointments at work that kept me busy. It was a normal morning at the hotel with the usual check-ins, and while I didn't normally man the reception desk, I happened to be behind the counter when someone cleared their throat.

"Hello, I'm Wilson Curtis," he said. "I have a reservation."

I looked up at the customer then, to find exactly what I didn't even know I'd been looking for. Tall, brown hair, kind eyes, and a southern accent that crept along my skin like warm fingers. I had to remind myself what I was doing. *Shit. I should be checking him in... Not checking him out...*

"Ah, yes," I said, bringing the booking up on screen. "Curtis and Mackey. We've been expecting you."

He frowned and mumbled, "Actually, it's just Curtis. The Mackey half isn't coming."

Shit. It wouldn't be the first time we've had the dejected half of a couple turn up alone. But God, there really was something about this guy that had me staring. He had a country-boy charm and damn, that accent... I'd definitely have to point him out to Adam.

Normally one of the reception staff would show customers to their rooms, but I wanted to do the honors. Truthfully, I just wanted to spend a little more time with him. "I'll show you to your room."

I did exactly that and gave him a rundown of the hotel while he took in the room, looking lost and overwhelmed. He'd said he was here alone, and it didn't sound like it was entirely his choice, so I tried to make him feel more relaxed.

"Not all our guests come here with a partner," I started, realizing I'd just dove head first into personal, unprofessional territory. Not exactly the *personal, unprofessional territory* I had in mind... I really needed to point this guy out to Adam. I didn't know what it was about him, but something sparked for me. This guy was different.

I told him to enjoy his stay before leaving his room and instead of going back to my office, I walked straight to the bar.

Adam grinned at me. "Hey. Wassup?"

"Room number seven," I murmured. "His name is Wilson. He's here by himself."

It took a moment for Adam to clue in as to why I was telling him this. His eyebrows raised. "You think he's all right?"

"I do. There's something about him."

He nodded nonchalantly. "Then I'll check him out."

"There he is," I whispered, nodding in the direction of Wilson, who was walking off toward the beach.

Adam stared at him for a long moment, and it was only when he was out of sight that Adam looked back at me. "He's here by himself?"

"Yep. Not too sure, but I think his boyfriend bailed on him."

A slow smile spread across Adam's face. He looked at me. "Well, it seems like we've found our man."

"If he's willing," I amended.

Adam gave me his everybody-loves-me grin. "Oh, he will be." I laughed and he nudged his hip to mine. "You so want him."

I couldn't deny it. "I do."

"Then you shall get what you want." He kissed me quickly and went back to his work but smiling more genuinely now. The smile that had been absent these last few weeks was back. I hoped like hell this Wilson guy was up for some holiday-threesome fun. There was something about him—from my, albeit, two minutes with him earlier—that sang to me. I didn't know what it was about him, but I sure as hell wanted to find out.

Later that afternoon when I was done in the office, I went back to reception to grab the days' receipts. Looking out across the lobby, I saw Wilson at the bar, laughing at something Adam had said, and I knew it was going to happen. Maybe not tonight, but soon. When we'd closed up for the night and Adam and I were in our apartment upstairs, he pulled me onto the sofa with him.

I leaned my back against his chest and he held me close, his lips at my ear. "I promise you, tomorrow night we'll have Wilson in our bed," he whispered. "He'll be between us and we can share him."

I craned my neck, giving him better access to the skin there. He kissed behind my ear and took my earlobe between his teeth. "I like him, Sy," he admitted. "You were right. There's something about him."

"Mmm." His hot breath was warming my blood. "You think he'll be interested?"

Adam chuckled. "Of course he will be."

I turned in his arms and pinned him to the sofa. His eyes widened, as did his smile, and I ground my hips against his. "I can't wait to have both of you."

Adam writhed under me. "Maybe once won't be enough with him."

"Maybe it won't," I conceded, kissing him. "Would you be okay with that?"

He laughed like the notion was ridiculously obvious. "You better believe I would be. Now quit your talking and put your mouth to better use."

I did exactly as he'd asked, but couldn't help wonder what this change meant, this wanting for a repeat with a man we hadn't even had once. Though this Wilson Curtis, this beautiful stranger, was only staying for two weeks... How different could it be?

CHAPTER ONE

WILSON

The foyer of the hotel was beautiful. The furniture matched the dark hardwood floors and beams, white walls and the cathedral ceiling. It reminded me of pictures I'd seen in brochures for Tahiti, not really what I'd expected from a hotel in Key West.

Not that I'd really known *what* to expect. I'd never left Alabama before. My first vacation out of state was supposed to have been for two—a romantic two weeks, secluded, private, and intimate. With a resigned sigh, I dropped my bags at the reception desk.

The man who looked up at me was tall with short, black, spiky hair, sky-blue eyes and a beautiful, full-lipped but professional smile. His name tag declared him to be Simon.

"Hello, I'm Wilson Curtis," I told him. "I have a reservation."

"Ah, yes," he said, typing on his keyboard. "Curtis and Mackey. We've been expecting you."

I swallowed down the lump in my throat. "Actually, it's just Curtis. The Mackey half isn't coming."

I tried to look like it didn't bother me, like it was my choice to be here solo, but my faltering smile must have given me away. Simon stared at me for a long, uncomfortable second before seeming to remember his professional position. He handed me a key and said, "I'll show you to your room."

I'd chosen the smaller, more personal hotel for the privacy. There were only twelve rooms in all—that would have ensured we'd be left alone and not be under the prying eyes of too many others. Not that it mattered. Not anymore. It was a gay-friendly hotel too, where we could have just been ourselves, without judgment, without fear.

Not that that mattered anymore either.

After walking out from behind the desk, Simon collected the bag from the floor near my feet. There was a smile in his eyes as he led me out through the foyer into a courtyard by the pool. "You're in room seven," he said, leading the way. There were small bungalow-style rooms off the pool, but the entire area opened out onto the sand and the Gulf of Mexico.

Simon smiled at my distraction at the view. "Restaurant is open noon till two for lunch, from six till ten for dinner. The bar is open from lunch till late." He waved his hand toward the poolside bar with a thatched roof.

He unlocked the door to my room, walked in, and put my bag on the bed. The room was decked out in white, with dark floors, and the only color was the lime-green painting above the bed—the huge, king-sized bed.

It was beautiful.

Simon cleared his throat to get my attention. His dark

hair, pale skin, and blue eyes made for an interesting combination. There was absolutely no doubt he was a good-looking guy. "Not all our guests come here with a partner," he said, somewhat diplomatically. "So please feel free to take a look around, and this afternoon, if you find yourself at the bar, you might find others who are... looking for company."

I blinked at his blatant assumption. "Uh..."

"Enjoy your stay," Simon added professionally. "And if you need anything, be sure to let me know. If I'm not here, any of the staff will help." And with another smile, he turned and walked out, closing the door behind him.

I sat on the bed and took a deep breath. This wasn't what it was supposed to be like. It wasn't the vacation I'd planned, but when Rod had told me he wouldn't be coming with me, I had two choices. I could either stay in Dalton, Alabama, and face an entire town full of people who had their homophobic pitchforks at the ready, or I could come to Key West and take the vacation by myself.

So that was just what I'd done.

Leaving my business in the trusted hands of my best friend, Callie, I'd packed my bag, boarded a plane in Birmingham, and sat next to an empty seat the entire way to Key West, Florida, for a two-week vacation.

By myself.

I had no intention of spending the two weeks wallowing in self-pity. What was the point? Rod had made himself clear. We were through. And the more I thought about it, the more I wondered whether there had ever been an *us* at all.

So I unpacked my things and set off to have a look around.

The hotel opened directly onto the beach, so it seemed

the logical place to start. I kicked off my shoes, hit the sand in bare feet, and walked.

It was cathartic. The ocean, even without waves, still had an ebb and flow, a rhythm to it—it was cleansing. The blue sky looked better over the blue of the Gulf. I didn't know why, but *life* looked better when viewed over the blue of the ocean.

It looked... simpler.

After I'd walked for long enough, feeling the hot sand and cool water on my feet, I found myself, just as Simon had suggested, sitting at the bar.

I waited until the bartender had finished serving the two guys before me. Nothing here seemed urgent. The bartender had a mop of unruly blond hair, a square jaw, sun-kissed skin, blue-green eyes, and a contagious smile.

"Adam," he introduced himself.

I smiled back at him and returned the courtesy. "Wilson Curtis."

"What can I get you, Wil?"

Wil. There was only one other person who called me that. "Just a soda, thanks."

He raised an eyebrow—I think my non-alcoholic drink choice threw him—but he served me with a smile. He joked that he didn't think boys with a Southern accent like mine drank *just soda*. I rolled my eyes at him, and he laughed. I soon learned Adam always smiled. He had an honest face. His smile made me smile.

He was quick to greet other guys, serving them cocktails and easy conversation, but always came back to me. Whether he was taking pity on me because I was there alone or he was just excellent at his job, I didn't know.

Over the next two days, I took in the sights of Key West during the day, went for walks along the beach in the afternoon and sat at the bar and talked to Adam at night. Simon joined us when he finished his shift each night and slid straight into the conversation. We discussed all sorts of things, from current affairs to movies, music and sports, but the conversations between us were fun and flirty.

The first time Simon walked behind the bar and kissed Adam, I almost died of heart failure. They were boyfriends, apparently. Adam chuckled at my reaction. I'd never seen guys kiss in front of me before, and I'd almost choked on my drink.

Simon was more standoffish than Adam, but he wasn't snobby. He was just quieter than the always-smiling, make-me-laugh Adam. They were an interesting couple, not that I was any kind of expert on gay couples, but it was easy to tell they adored each other. There was always a quick kiss, a touch on the arm, a smile. It was something I'd never experienced, and I envied them that. It really was beautiful to watch.

The resort itself was perfect—small, private, and very, *very* open. There were gay couples everywhere, men kissing, men dancing. It was a little shocking at first for me. I'd never been exposed to such open public displays of affection between men. But I fucking loved it.

At night, alone in my huge, king-sized bed, I would jerk off to images of other men holding hands, kissing, fucking. I hoped by the time my two weeks were up, I would have found someone to share that with, even if just for one night. And I was pretty damn sure by the time my two weeks were up, I wouldn't want to leave.

Certainly not to go back to my homophobic hometown.

On the third day, by late afternoon, I found myself back at the bar. Sure, I'd chatted with other guys, but I kept coming back to my favorite bartender. I knew he was taken, but there was something about him that just drew me in. He joked and laughed, and even when some other guys tried to strike up conversation, I preferred to stay and talk to Adam.

"So what's your story?" he asked with a grin as he handed me a beer. "You come to a gay hotel alone, you don't drink much, and when that guy tried to pick you up just now, you declined?"

I blinked at him. "Pick me up?" I looked back at the guy who'd just left the bar, and sure enough, he was talking to someone else and seemed to be having better luck. "Oh. I hope I didn't offend him."

That only made Adam chuckle louder and shake his head. "Oh, Wil, you are a doll."

Simon walked in behind the bar and smiled at Adam. "What's so funny?"

"Oh, hey," Adam greeted him warmly. "Wil here was just making me laugh."

Simon looked at me, then at Adam, and they seemed to have some silent exchange before Simon kissed him, then looked back at me and smiled. "So, Wil..."

I stared at them. I still wasn't used to seeing two men kiss in front of me. Sure, I'd seen porn, I'd seen movies, but before I'd come to Key West, it'd never happened *right* in front of me. "Um, yeah?"

Simon walked around to my side of the bar and sat on a stool at the end, a few feet from me. "Do you dance?"

"Do I what?"

Adam laughed, making me look at him. He nodded pointedly over my shoulder toward the open foyer where there were people dancing.

Couples, slow-dancing.

Men.

Men slow-dancing with other men. Oh my God... I'd

never seen anything like it. Not in front of me, not with my own two eyes.

I looked back at Adam, then Simon. The amazement must have been obvious on my face because they both grinned at me. "Uh, n-n-no," I stammered. "No, I don't dance."

"That's a shame," Adam said wistfully. I finished my beer. I kept looking over my shoulder to the dancing men. They were... mesmerizing.

Simon cleared his throat, making me look at him. "So," he said, "what brought you to Key West?"

I sighed and Adam served me a fresh bottle of beer. I took a sip and a deep breath, then I told them. I told them everything.

How my life in Dalton had gone to hell. My quiet, peaceful, boring, *closeted* life wasn't so closeted anymore.

How one comment was all it had taken to end everything. Well, one comment, inquisitive minds, and the grapevine that was Dalton. Quiet whispers had spread like wildfire and the small town was having none of it.

I explained how I had been sitting at a table in the bar with the guys I always had a beer with after work when two guys I'd gone to high school with had spotted me. They'd been drunk and even more obnoxious than they'd been ten years before. As they'd stumbled past our table, they'd seen me and laughed.

"Look, it's the kitchen fairy," one had said.

The other man had corrected him, "You mean it's the kitchen fag."

I'd laughed them off as redneck losers who didn't have an IQ between them higher than their boot size, and the other guys had kind of laughed too. But Rod hadn't. He'd just sat there.

"Deputy to the Chief of Police, Rod Mackey, just fucking sat there."

"Who's Rod?" Adam asked.

"The guy I'd been seeing," I said. "Secretly. For two years."

"Two *years*?" Simon asked. "And he didn't say *anything*?"

I shook my head. "We were all hush-hush. No one knew we were gay, let alone seeing each other."

Both Simon and Adam stared at me.

I sighed again. "So the man who should have said something just sat there. Even out of his uniform, it wouldn't have seemed out of place if he'd reprimanded those two assholes. In uniform, he *should* have reprimanded them." I took another pull of my beer. "But he couldn't. Or so he told me afterward. He called me later that night to tell me we were over. He couldn't risk it, he said. He told me if he'd made a scene with those two guys in the bar, it would've looked suspicious."

Adam's eyes narrowed, and Simon huffed. "What did the other guys at the table do?"

"John and Danny thought it was suspicious Rod *didn't* say something. They called him on it, asking if he'd gone soft, and he just sat there." I shook my head. "He didn't know where to look. He certainly didn't look at me."

"What happened after that?" Adam asked quietly.

"They just sat back and blinked a few times, looking at me. I tried to shrug it off, saying I'd always been pegged as different in high school because I'd never played football. I'm a chef. So fucking what?"

"You're a chef?" Simon asked.

I nodded. "Yep."

Adam looked at me, concerned. "What did those guys do? Those John and Danny guys... did they hurt you?"

"What?" *Hurt me?* "No, nothing like that," I reassured him. "No, they just sat there, finished their beers, and without so much as another word, they got up and left. I saw it in their eyes, that they'd put it together. I'd never had a girlfriend, never hooked up with girls..." I shook my head slowly as I remembered. "Then Rod sat there for a beat too long, snatched his coat off the back of his chair, and followed them while I sat there wondering what the hell had just happened."

I finished my beer and told them, "The next day, when I went to the store to collect my daily order of fresh produce, old Mr. Bryant refused to serve *my type*."

"Your *type*?" Simon repeated.

I nodded. "That would be gay."

"Oh my God," Simon whispered.

Adam handed me another beer—my third—and I took a drink. "To say I was shocked is an understatement, but then it went downhill as the day went on. We had people canceling reservations and some just not show up." I barked out a laugh, though it was anything but funny. "One group who did have the courtesy to call and cancel told Callie—she's my best friend and sous chef—it was because they didn't want to catch being gay from my food."

Of all the ridiculous, ludicrous, and hurtful things.

"I'm really sorry," Adam said quietly.

I looked at him. He had an expression of genuine regret on his face, as if it was something he understood. I gave him a sad smile. "It wasn't the names they called me that bothered me the most. It wasn't even the fact Rod dumped me. It was the fact my restaurant, my business, was leverage. They knew if my business went bad, I'd have no choice but to leave. Either way, they'd win."

Simon stood up and walked behind the bar and kissed the side of Adam's head. He whispered something in his ear, and Adam smiled.

Adam walked around to my side of the bar and grabbed my hand. "Come on," he said. And without giving me a chance to argue, he pulled me to my feet.

"What are you doing?"

Adam laughed. *"You're* going to dance."

"Here?" I asked incredulously. We were standing at the bar! I turned to look at the other men who were dancing, only to find them gone. "But no one else is dancing," I told him, and he looked at me and grinned.

"And no one else can see us," he said simply.

Realizing he wasn't going to let me get out of this, I spun around to look at Adam's boyfriend. "Um... Simon..."

Adam slipped his arm around my waist and pulled me closer. "Simon doesn't mind, believe me."

He was an inch or two shorter than my six-foot-one, but I could feel his chest against mine and his hands on my back, holding me to him. I could feel the heat of his body. I could smell him... Then Adam started to move his feet, just side to side in a swaying motion. I'd never danced with a man before, much less slow-danced with a man while his boyfriend watched.

It was heady. I'd only had three beers, but my head was swimming.

I could feel Simon's gaze on me and found myself looking back at him. It was obviously okay for Adam to dance with another man because Simon looked rather pleased. In fact, he looked a little smug.

When he walked over to us, I froze. But he stepped

right up to us and kissed Adam soundly, and I gasped in shock. Holy hell, it was one thing to see a man kiss another man, but to see two men kiss when one of them had his arms around me... *Jesus*.

Simon walked away, and Adam tightened his embrace and whispered into my neck, "Is this okay?"

All I could do was nod.

"Does it feel good?"

My heart was hammering, and I nodded again.

"Did Ron-what's-his-name ever make you feel good?"

I didn't bother correcting his name. Did Rod ever make me feel good? Did I come? Yes. But did he ever make me feel desired? Wanted? Well, no... No, he didn't.

I must have taken too long to answer because Adam stopped moving and pulled back to look at me. "Did he?"

I shook my head. "No. Not really."

Adam pulled me against him again and shook his head. "Now that's a terrible shame."

I noticed then that Simon was turning off lights and closing and locking doors. When the music stopped, I figured the dance was over.

But Adam never stopped moving. In fact, he held me tighter.

He dug his fingers into my skin, and pressed his body against me. I could *feel* him, all of him. I had no doubt he could feel me, what he did to me, how hard I was. And when he snaked his hand down my back, over my ass, and pulled our hips together, I *knew* he could feel how hard I was.

Then Simon was next to us. I should have been alarmed, but I wasn't. And when he put his arm on my lower back, I should have shied away, but I didn't.

I welcomed it.

And when Simon stepped behind me, slow and close against my back, I should have said stop. But I didn't.

I moaned.

Adam pulled back a little to look me in the eyes. He never spoke. He didn't have to. But he was silently asking me if this was okay, if I wanted him to stop. So I dug my fingers into his skin to hold him a little tighter as my answer. He smiled then trailed his lips over my neck, kissing over my jaw, and asked with a gruff whisper, "What do you want? What do you want to feel?"

"I want to feel desired... wanted." The words were out before I could stop them.

Simon's hands moved to my hips and his lips came close to my ear. "We can show you what that feels like."

As both men pressed against me, sandwiching me while Adam kissed my exposed neck, I let my head fall back onto Simon's shoulder. I uncurled my arm from around Adam's back to pull my room key from my pocket. I tried to find the words to tell them what I wanted, what I needed, but I was panting and could only say one word.

"Please."

CHAPTER TWO

OH, fuck...

I'd never known anything like it.

Two mouths on me, four hands, two bodies surrounding me, devouring me, consuming me. The push and pull, the desire...

Fuck.

We somehow made it to my room, and as soon as I walked through the door, Adam was on me.

"Goddammit," he mumbled as he kissed down my neck, his mouth open and wet, his fingers digging into my sides.

Simon closed the door then stood behind me again. He kissed the back of my neck down to my shoulder. His hands skimmed over my back and pulled my shirt up and over my head. I was suddenly half-naked between two men with their hands all over me. I didn't see where he threw my shirt. I didn't fucking care.

I groaned. "Oh God."

Adam leaned down to trail his mouth over my chest, licking and sucking as he went. I ran my hands through his hair, guiding him, encouraging him, and when he took my nipple between his lips, I couldn't help but arch into him.

Simon moaned behind me, his breath warm against my ear. Letting go of one fistful of Adam's hair, I reached back to take a handful of Simon's. He pushed against me, rubbing himself against my ass while he skimmed his hands over my stomach. He pressed hot, open-mouth kisses over my neck, my shoulder, my ear.

When Adam kissed back up my chest and over my collarbone, his lips found Simon's and they kissed. Like I wasn't wedged between them, like I didn't have a hand in both men's hair. They pushed against me, one at the front, one at the back, trying to get closer as their mouths melded together above my shoulder.

God, I wanted to kiss them. Both of them. My mouth hung open, wanting, panting.

When they broke the kiss, Adam whispered, "Oh, Sy, I want him."

What, was he asking for Simon's permission?

Before I could ask, Simon must have answered, because Adam kissed me. Deep, hard, lips, and tongue, he commanded the kiss. Just like I wanted. Just how I needed.

Without waiting for us to stop kissing, Simon spoke into my ear, "Do you want this, Wil?"

I pulled my mouth from Adam's. All I could do was nod. Yes. Yes, I wanted it. So fucking much.

Simon whispered, "Do you want just one or both of us?"

Fuck.

"Both," I panted. "Please, both."

Adam smiled and his eyes darkened as he licked his swollen lips. Simon reached between Adam and me and unbuttoned my cargos. *Oh, fuck.*

My cock ached, desperate for friction, for anything. I stepped out of my shorts, and after I'd toed off my shoes, Adam pulled on my hand, leading me toward the bed. When my legs hit the mattress, he pushed against me, forcing me backward until I was lying down.

He crawled up over my legs, kissing as he went. He stopped when he got to my briefs. Looking up at me, he tongued my cock through the material. I let my head fall back against the bed and savored the sensations curling through my body. *Oh, fuck.*

"Condoms?" Simon's voice startled me.

I looked over at him. His shirt was unbuttoned and untucked. I could see his defined stomach and chest. I think I licked my lips because he smiled. "Condoms?"

"Um, yes," I stammered. I looked to the bedside table. "Top drawer."

Adam pulled my briefs down, freeing my straining cock. He licked up my entire length, flicking his tongue at the tip.

I gripped the bedspread and closed my eyes. "Oh, Jesus."

Then he was gone.

I lifted my head to find Adam grinning at me as he pulled his shirt over his head. I was lying on the bed, naked except for my briefs around my thighs. Adam quickly undid his pants and, leaving his briefs on, knelt on the bed beside me.

Simon stood in front of us.

"Are you ready, Wil?" Simon was leading this. His blue eyes were intense and serious, a stark contrast to Adam's bright smile. "Because this is how we're gonna do this."

I swallowed hard at his tone, his authority. He threw a handful of condoms on the bed beside us and took his shirt all the way off. "Adam's gonna bend over this bed and you're gonna fuck him," he said.

I gasped at his words.

"And while you're buried in him, I'm going to fuck you," he said, and my whole body shivered.

Adam leaned over me, looking down at me. His hair flopped forward and he smiled. "Is that okay?"

My breaths were labored. "But I've never topped."

Adam blinked. "Never?"

I shook my head, and he leaned down to kiss me softly before pulling back.

"But you want to?"

I lifted my head off the bed to peck my lips against his, and I nodded. Then I looked over at Simon, who was staring at us on the bed, and I told him, "Yeah. I want to."

Simon smiled, then looked at Adam. "Get him ready."

Adam scooted off the bed and pulled me to the edge of the mattress by my legs. Quickly pulling my briefs off, he lifted my legs, exposing my ass to him. I closed my eyes, expecting the familiar feel of fingers, waiting for the intrusion I so badly craved.

But the next thing I felt wasn't fingers at all.

I opened my eyes and looked down to see Adam with his flattened tongue, licking and pressing against my ass. His wet, hot tongue press into me. *Oh, God. Oh, fuck!* He was fucking me with his tongue. I'd never... I'd never... never like that.

I couldn't *not* watch. It was mesmerizing. Adam stood leaning over me, with his mouth on me, working me, fucking me with his tongue, while Simon stood behind him. I realized a little belatedly Simon was prepping Adam while Adam prepped me.

Jesus, this was going to happen. This was really going to happen.

Then Adam's mouth was gone, replaced by one finger, then another. *Oh God.* He licked my balls and tongued me while his fingers stretched me. There were sounds of wanton moans, and I could feel my release building, building... and when I begged for *more, more, please more,* Adam pulled out.

I looked up at him. "What are you...?"

Adam smiled and said, "Stand up."

Oh. When I scrambled off the bed to my feet, Adam took my face in his hands and kissed me. He plunged his tongue into my mouth, and I could taste me. It was a shock at first, but when he pulled away, I found myself wanting more.

Adam chuckled but then picked up a foil wrapper off the bed. Quickly opening it, he rolled the condom down the length of my cock, making me groan. And when he slicked me with lube and pumped me twice, I bucked into his hand.

"God, I'm gonna come so quick."

"No, you won't," Simon said roughly at my shoulder, making me jump. I'd almost forgotten he was there. "You'll wait until I'm inside you before you come. I want to *feel* it when you come."

His light blue eyes had turned dark and intense. They matched the tenor of his voice. I licked my lips and nodded. Simon pulled my chin between his thumb and forefinger and kissed me, sweeping his tongue into my mouth as though he were trying to taste Adam's mouth on mine. When he pulled away, he smiled.

When I turned back to face Adam, he was leaning over the bed, offering his ass to me. *Oh God.* My cock throbbed at the realization, at the very thought of what I was about to do. I put my hand on Adam's lower back and stood behind him, aligning my cock with his hole.

Simon moved to stand beside us, his eyes fixed on where we would join. "Okay, Wil, he's ready. Push into him."

So I did.

Holy fucking hell.

He was so tight. So fucking tight. I inched inside him, slowly, surely, and my cock felt as if it were made of steel. I gripped Adam's hips and groaned as I slid all the way in, making him groan and grip the bedspread.

I was lost to the sensation of it—how it felt, how it drew me in, how Adam moaned, how I trembled with need. Simon pulled my face toward him, distracting me from my orgasm. He was now naked. I hadn't noticed him undress. I stared at his hard-on. His long, condom-covered cock stood proudly from his body. I just stared at it, knowing where it was just about to go and wondering how far it would reach inside me.

Simon lifted my chin so I looked at him, and he kissed me. His voice was low when he whispered, "Breathe, Wil."

I sucked back a breath, and keeping his hand on my shoulder, Simon moved in behind me.

"Spread your legs," he told me, and without pulling out of Adam, I did as instructed. "Now keep still."

The blunt head of his cock pushed against my ass, and as he sank his fingers into the skin at my hips, he sank into me.

Oh, fuck. Oh, fuck.

Simon groaned as he pushed into me. I could feel every inch of him slowly sliding inside. The stretch, the burn, the pain soon became pleasure and my cock throbbed in the depth of Adam's ass.

Simon panted in my ear. "You ready for me to fuck you both?"

Adam moaned and clawed at the bedcovers. "God, yes, move. Please, Sy, move."

He needed it as much as I did. I needed to move, too.

This dual sensation was too much—my cock buried in Adam while Simon was buried in me. Every inch of Simon's long cock filled me, and when he pulled out and slammed back in, I fucked Adam. I slid out and slammed back into him as Simon did the same to me.

"How does that feel?" Simon groaned against the back of my neck.

"So fucking good," Adam whimpered. "So fucking good."

I was surrounded by them. Both Simon and Adam, everywhere, all at once.

I'd never been inside anyone before. It was hot and tight and pulsing and so, so fucking good. And when Simon's thrusts got faster, deeper, harder, and his grunts became louder, harsher, I couldn't take any more. He was fucking us both, both of us at the same time. It was too much and never enough.

And right. It was so fucking right.

Gripping his hips, I pushed Adam into the mattress, sliding into him, every inch of me, while I was being filled just the same by Simon. I'd never felt so wanted, so desired, so consumed. My cock swelled and stiffened inside Adam.

"Fuck, fuck, gonna come."

My orgasm detonated low in my belly, and white atomic heat barreled through me. I flexed into Adam with a final thrust as Simon drilled into me. My chest heaved forward and my head fell back as my cock erupted, spurting hot and thick into the condom.

Adam groaned loudly, "Yes. God, yes." And his ass clenched around me, again and again, squeezing the cum out of me as he came.

I bucked at the sensation. My body moved of its own accord as Adam writhed underneath me. Simon's hands dug into my sides, and he slammed into me once, twice, and with a gruff roar, he stilled over me. I could feel the surge of his cock in my ass as he came. So powerful, so perfect.

Underneath me, on top of me, inside me, inside him. It was a pleasure like I'd never known. So... complete.

There was no other word for it.

Complete.

Adam chuckled underneath me, rousing me from the haze in my brain. Simon kissed my shoulder, then pulled out of me, so I did the same to Adam. Condom dealt with, I stood up straight, and Adam pulled me up onto the bed. I fell against the pillows, and he settled himself half over me. "How was that for you?"

I snorted. "Um..."

Adam chuckled again. "It's amazing, isn't it?"

My skin was still tingling, my bones still spongy, and I wondered if my smile matched Adam's. I sighed and nodded. "Something like that."

He grinned even wider as Simon came out of the bathroom. "You've never done anything like that before, have you?"

I shook my head and answered quietly, "No."

Simon knelt on the bed and crawled over to us. He leaned in and kissed Adam soundly, right over my chest. "Are you okay?"

"Better than okay," Adam replied with a smirk. "That was fucking hot."

Simon looked at me then. "Do you feel okay?"

I smiled at his concern. It was easy to tell he was the serious one of the two. "I've never been better," I reassured him.

Adam buzzed with excitement. "Wil was just saying he's never done anything like this." He motioned his hand between the three of us. "So maybe we should extend the offer for the rest of his stay."

Simon blinked at his boyfriend's words, and even in the darkened room, I could tell he was surprised. Before he could answer, Adam kept talking. "Come on, Sy. You know you want to." He leaned up on his arm, pulled Simon's chin toward him, and kissed him softly, a few inches from my face. "I know you're already thinking of all the things you'd like to do to both of us."

Simon groaned and looked down at me, then back to Adam. "Well, he is kinda cute."

Adam grinned and bounced, then abruptly stopped. "Oh." He stared at me, his smile long gone. "Oh, only if you want to, Wil..."

I snorted. As if I wouldn't want to experience that again. "Oh, I want to." I looked at Simon. "If it's okay with you?"

Simon checked us both, rolled his eyes, and smirked. I took that as a yes.

I looked at Adam, and the smile he gave me was beautiful. I leaned up off the bed and Adam kissed me, open-mouthed, with teasing tongue and smiling, swollen lips. And when he pulled away from me, he kissed Simon.

It was amazing to watch them kiss, all soft lips, gentle tongues, and whimpers. And the fact they were naked in my bed with me, kissing just two inches from my face, was surreal.

Simon pulled his mouth from Adam's, only to press his lips to mine. His kiss was lazy and languid, soft and sweet.

Then Adam joined in.

The three of us kissed. It was bizarre to have two other mouths, two other tongues all tangling together, two pairs of hands, two other bodies. It was such a turn-on. It was beautiful.

And my cock stirred.

"Oh, fuck," I groaned and fell back on the bed. They both looked at me questioningly. I gave a laugh and reached down to give my dick a squeeze. "These next ten days are gonna kill me."

Adam laughed and leaned down to peck my lips with his. "You won't ever want to leave."

I was about to tell him he was probably right, but he put my mouth to better use by kissing me again while Simon kissed down my ribs. Both men lay down next to me, half on top of me, and within minutes, the three of us were a writhing, moaning mess on the bed.

Going back to Alabama was the last thing on my mind.

CHAPTER THREE

I WOKE up to a nose nudging the back of my head. "Hey, sleepyhead."

I opened my eyes to find it was barely daylight and Adam was smiling at me.

"Wassup?" I croaked.

"We're heading home," Adam said. It was then I noticed he was dressed. "We didn't want you to wake up and think we'd just left."

I rolled over to see Simon was getting dressed.

"It's a quarter to six in the morning," Simon told me as he buttoned up his shirt. "We'd better head out before the whole hotel wakes up."

Adam playfully slapped my ass. "And I gotta go to church."

"Church?" I repeated, my voice still thick from sleep. I scrubbed my hands over my face. "What day is it?"

"It's Monday," Simon chuckled. "Adam's church is open every day."

Adam's grin widened, then he looked at me. "Go back to sleep. We'll see you later."

"Mmm," I hummed, still half-asleep.

Adam chuckled, and I couldn't help but smile back at him. He leaned over and kissed my cheek. "Can't wait for tonight."

Simon shook his head apologetically before he pulled Adam off the bed. "Come on. Leave him be. He's on vacation." Then he looked at me and said, "I'll see you at breakfast."

They left and I lay there, stretched out in the rumpled king-sized bed by myself. It smelled of us. What we'd done last night. Twice. How we'd fucked the first time over the side of the bed, me buried in Adam, Simon buried in me. Then how the three of us had lain on the bed kissing and touching until we'd formed a triangle, giving and getting blow jobs.

It had been amazing. It had been better than amazing.

I tried not to think about the dynamics or what it meant. I just decided to go with the flow. I mean, why not? It was just for ten days. So for the next ten days, I would fuck and be fucked as much as my body could stand, then go back to Alabama, my failing business, and what was left of my miserable life.

If ten days was all I got, I was going to make the most of it.

I rolled over and pulled the pillow under my head. The more I thought of Adam and Simon, the more I smiled. They were so different, yet so compatible. It had been hard not to like Adam from the moment I'd met him. He had a charm to him, a magnetism. Simon, on the other hand, was more reserved. At first he seemed snobbish and cold, but then he'd smile at me and warm me all the way through.

Simon seemed to be the one who reined in Adam's enthusiasm. He was the responsible one, the one who took care of Adam, and it seemed that Adam needed it, even liked it.

But Adam was the one who breathed life into them, who kept Simon on his toes. Like Adam was a teenager and Simon was the adult, despite both being in their mid-twenties, just a few years younger than me.

They were the perfect balance.

I knew it had been Adam's idea to include me. They'd all but said so. So even if Simon included me at Adam's insistence, I didn't mind. Even if Simon tolerated me only because his boyfriend wanted to play threesomes for ten days, I'd take it.

He hadn't seemed to mind being balls-deep in my ass last night. Or when I'd taken his dick in my mouth and swallowed everything he gave me. He hadn't minded at all.

I smiled at the realization they'd slept in my bed. We'd fallen asleep with Adam in the middle, all touching, all sated. And they'd stayed, only to wake me when they were leaving so I didn't think they'd just fucked me and left.

As the room filled with sunlight, I got up, showered, dressed, then went in search of coffee. The morning staff were professional and friendly. In fact, the morning kitchen staff were friendlier than the evening shift. It was easy to tell from only three days here by his attitude toward his food and toward his staff that the head chef was an arrogant ass. There was no respect in his dishes and no cohesion in the ingredients he used.

The display of fresh fruit, croissants, and coffee was perfect. There were other couples already seated, all bright-eyed and in love. The men looked adoringly at each other across the tables, and being the only single guy there, I took my tray to the far table overlooking the beach.

Sipping my coffee, I pulled out my phone and dialed

the only person back home who was talking to me. Despite it being just on breakfast time, my best friend answered on the third ring.

"Hello?"

"Hey, Callie."

"Hey, you," she replied. It was so good to hear her voice, even after only a few days. "How's Florida?"

"It's, um... it's great," I answered, still grinning. "How's the restaurant?"

"Restaurant's okay," she said dismissively. "Elaborate on *great*. You sound awfully cheery."

I guess compared to the miserable state I'd been in when I'd left, I must've sounded a lot happier. I sipped my coffee and sighed.

"It's been wonderful," I told her, not really sure how much I should divulge. Callie had always known I was gay, and that Rod and I were secretly seeing each other, but I'd never discussed details, not about what we did anyway.

"You're not down there all by your lonesome, are you?"

My mind went straight to Adam and Simon. "No, I'm not alone..."

Callie gasped. "Did you meet someone?"

It wasn't like I could explain that I'd met two someones, but still, I couldn't help but grin. "Something like that."

Then she squealed. "When you get home, I want details. You hear me, Wil Curtis?"

I laughed her off, and changed the subject. "Now about the restaurant... How's it going?"

"Yeah, it's been okay," she answered vaguely, trailing off with a mumbled sound.

"Callie, please." I stopped her midsentence. "Just answer me honestly. Have people been coming back?"

"Well, yes..."

"Well, yes, what? That wasn't very convincing, Cal."

She sighed. "Wil, can we talk about it when you get back? You're on vacation."

I knew what she wasn't telling me. I knew her too well. "Callie, will I even have a business to come back to?"

And her too-long silence was my answer.

I ran my hand through my hair and sighed, resigned. "Jesus Christ, Cal."

"I know," she said softly. "It'll be all right, Wil. Everything will work out, you'll see."

I huffed out a laugh. "Since when did you become so philosophical?"

Callie laughed with me and told me to enjoy the rest of my vacation, and she'd call me in a day or two. She never mentioned Rod, if she'd seen him or spoken to him, and I didn't ask. I just didn't want to know.

When I hung up, Simon sat down beside me, dressed in his work uniform and holding coffee. "Everything okay back home?"

I gave a loud sigh. "Not really. But I don't have to worry about it for ten days, right?"

Simon gave a small nod, then sipped his coffee. He looked out toward the waveless ocean and nodded pointedly toward one swimmer in particular. "He looks good out there."

I'd never really paid much attention to the swimmers before. There were always people swimming along the shoreline, but I looked out at the water, then back to Simon. The way he kept watching one particular person made me take another look. "Is that Adam?"

Simon smiled and nodded. "Swims every morning."

"I thought he said he was going to church?"

Simon chuckled quietly. "The ocean is his church. He

swims and snorkels—non-stop if you let him. He finds his peace there."

I looked from Simon to Adam, a few hundred yards away. He was now walking out of the water, and when I turned back to look at Simon, he was watching Adam too. There was nothing but love in his blue eyes and a small smile on his lips as he watched Adam walk toward us.

It made me smile too.

I wanted to ask him questions, like how long had they been together? How had they met? Had there been other single guys who they'd taken to bed? How many had there been? And why me?

Sure, I was here by myself. Maybe I was a little naïve and an easy target. But why *me*? Why not pick some other guy? Why not pick a couple and make it four?

But when Simon raised his eyebrows at me, questioning my staring at him, I couldn't do it. I don't know why. He'd have answered me honestly, but maybe I'd feel more comfortable asking Adam. So instead I asked, "Where do you live? I mean, it must be close by..." I trailed off, almost regretting my choice of question.

Simon gave a pointed glance to the second floor of the hotel. "Up there. Manager's residence."

"You're the manager of this place?" I asked.

Simon smiled. "Yep. For almost three years."

"Wow." I couldn't hide my surprise. "It's a big respon-sibility."

He nodded. "The owners don't come by much, so I'm the day-to-day manager. I make all decisions, run staff, and manage the hotel itself. They just have their names and bank accounts behind it."

"Still," I conceded, "it's a great place. You do a great job."

Simon gave me a half smirk. "Thanks. But you're the same as me. You run your own business."

I turned my phone over in my hands and threw it on the table. "Well, maybe not for too much longer."

"Is it that bad?" he asked quietly.

I sighed. "I won't know for sure till I go home, but apparently being gay is bad for business."

Simon's jaw clenched and he shook his head. "What will you do?"

It wasn't like I could admit to not having a clue. Being a chef was my life. My business was my entire life. It was all I knew. I'd worked long and hard for everything it stood for, and now it hung by a thread. I shrugged, unsure of how to answer. "Guess I'll find out in nine days."

Simon nodded again and sipped his coffee. "Mmm, nine days," he said, almost to himself. "We'd better make each one of them worth your while."

I let out a nervous laugh. "I was thinking that very thing."

"What were you just thinking?" Adam's voice startled me. I'd been watching Simon and hadn't seen Adam come up the stone steps toward us. He was decked out in wetsuit shorts and was rubbing a towel through his floppy wet hair.

Simon smiled warmly at his boyfriend. "We were just saying we need to make the most of the next nine days."

Oh my God. They were going to talk about this openly. In all my time with Rod, we'd never discussed anything we did.

Adam gave us both a pointed stare. "You damn well better not be planning anything that doesn't include me."

I barked out a laugh, and Simon chuckled as he stood up. "Wouldn't dream of it." He gave me a warm smile and walked off toward the kitchen.

I looked at Adam, to find him looking at me and smiling. Always smiling. "So what's your plan for the day?" he asked.

"Not sure. Might head into town again, have a look around," I told him. "Do the tourist thing."

Adam nodded. "It's a shame we have to work. We could go with you, show you the sights. Actually, I'm off work tomorrow and the next day. I can show you around then if you like."

I smiled at him. "That'd be great."

"Just be sure you're free tonight, okay? I'm sure Simon has something in mind for us to do." He raised his eyebrows suggestively and hummed. "Anyway, I better go get changed and get ready for work." He started to leave, but then stopped. "Oh, and we finish around eight or nine tonight, but anytime you want to sit at the bar and keep me company..." He didn't wait for me to answer. It was an implied request.

I bit my bottom lip, knowing damn well I would.

I watched him leave, saying "Hi" to a few other guests as he walked through the hotel. I collected my phone off the table and walked back to my room. It wasn't even eight in the morning and I was already wishing the day was over. I just wanted it to be eight at night, and I wanted to be in my bed with two men. And I really, really wanted to know what Simon had in mind for us to do.

CHAPTER FOUR

I DID SOME SIGHTSEEING, though I was somewhat distracted. The scenery was postcard-perfect—blue skies, even bluer water and sun-bleached sand. It couldn't have been any prettier. But my mind kept wandering to Adam and Simon.

I liked them.

I liked being with them. I liked their energy.

And it wasn't as though I liked one over the other, because I liked them *together*. I liked them as a unit. Even though I got the impression Simon only tolerated me for Adam's sake, I couldn't see myself being with Adam without Simon.

I tried not to think of my restaurant and Callie's comments to me earlier on the phone. It was the longest I'd ever spent away from my business since I started it two years ago. I'd rarely even had a day off.

I loved my work. I loved my business, having watched it grow from the beginning. My hard work and long hours had paid off. I'd honed my skills, learned what I could, and it showed. My restaurant was popular, always busy. It was my life.

Until a week ago.

And now, apparently, it was all but over.

I had no idea what I'd be going home to. No idea what I'd do when I got there. And the very worst of it was, I didn't know if I was even welcome. I knew damn well whatever Rod and I had was done, and I assumed my friendship with the likes of John and Danny was too.

But the clincher was, given the opportunity to go back in time to change being outed, I wasn't sure I would.

Sure, I wished my business wasn't in the toilet. I wished my only chance of a sexual relationship with another man in my hometown—and the memory of it—hadn't been rendered to nothing.

But now that I was out of the closet, I wasn't sure I'd want to go back. Regardless of the cost. Especially now that I'd seen how people like Adam and Simon lived, out in the open with nothing to hide.

I wanted that.

Would I ever have that in Dalton, Alabama?

"Hey," the bus driver called out, snapping me out of my thoughts. "This your stop?"

I looked out of the tour bus window to find I was already back at the hotel. My worries seemed to disappear when I walked into the lobby. The dark wood trim and white walls, open to the sunlight, made me smile. There were men, all couples, chatting and laughing and another couple in the pool.

It was like my very own private paradise.

For the next nine days, anyway.

I went straight to my room, changed into swim trunks, and hit the beach. The warm sand, cool water and mid-afternoon breeze were perfect for clearing my mind. By the time I walked back up the stone steps to the hotel, Adam was behind the bar, grinning at me.

I couldn't help but smile back at him. I walked over, rubbing a towel over my still-wet hair. "Hey."

He grinned beautifully. "How was your day?"

"Good. Saw some sights." I nodded. "I better go shower and get changed."

"That's a shame." Adam sighed. "I was just imagining licking the salt off your skin."

My mouth fell open at his blatant remark, and I could feel myself blush. I glanced around to see if anyone heard, but we were pretty much alone.

"Does that bother you?" he asked, still smiling.

I shook my head. "No, just not used to such forward comments."

"Mmm," he hummed. "There's a lot of things you're not used to. You'll have to tell me all the things your ex never did so we can remedy that."

I bit my bottom lip and gave him a shy smile. I cleared my throat, too inhibited to give details of what I'd done and what I wanted to do.

Adam chuckled and walked around to my side of the bar. He moved right up to me and smiled with darkened eyes. "So shy," he whispered, then slowly kissed my neck. "Mmm," he hummed again. "The salt of the ocean is sweet on your skin."

Fuck. I could feel his body heat. I could smell him. I shivered from head to foot.

Adam wagged his finger. "No jerking off in the shower. Wait till later, for Sy and me, okay?"

My breath caught, and all I could do was nod.

True to his request, I didn't jerk off in the shower. As

much as I ached and as hard as I was, I wanted to wait. I knew my release would be more intense if Adam and Simon were there, coaxing it out of me.

Sucking and fucking it out of me.

Dressed in jeans, a polo shirt, and the Keys' standard footwear of flip-flops, I went back out to the bar. There were other guys seated there and in the restaurant now, but being a Monday, it was quieter than the weekend had been.

Adam was talking to a couple, but he grinned when he saw me. "How was your shower?"

"Cold."

He barked out a laugh. "That's too bad."

I chuckled at him. "Yeah well, I figured it'd be, um, it'd be"—I looked at the other two guys at the bar next to me and cleared my throat, embarrassed—"in my best interest."

Adam laughed. "Oh, I'm sure it will be."

And it fucking was. I spent the evening at the bar, talking to some other guests, but mostly to Adam—and Simon when his work was done. They finished early, like they'd said they would, and by eight, I was on my bed with Simon buried to the hilt inside me and Adam's cock in my throat.

I came three times before midnight. It was worth the wait, indeed.

We fell asleep in a knotted mass of legs and arms, exhausted and thoroughly sated. And I woke to the feeling of being watched.

I opened my eyes to find it was Simon's gaze on me. He was on his side facing me, and Adam was between us, still asleep. I smiled at Simon, and when I looked at Adam's contented face, my smile widened.

"He looks happy," I whispered, my voice still thick from sleep.

Simon nodded, and there was a warm light in his eyes as he took in Adam's features. Then he looked at me. "You feel okay? You got quite the workout last night."

Before I could answer, an only-pretending-to-sleep Adam, still with his eyes closed, said, "He loved being worked out."

Simon laughed and strangely, I wasn't embarrassed. I dug my fingers into Adam's ribs, tickling him. "I thought you were asleep."

He squirmed and chuckled, wriggling his back against Simon, so they then both faced me. Simon draped his arm protectively around Adam, and they both smiled.

They looked so content, so happy. I wanted that. I wanted to be happy like that. Sure, I wanted the terrific sex, but I wanted the feeling of being so utterly loved.

I wanted what they had.

One day, I told myself. *One day.*

Simon sighed, bringing my attention back to them. "I gotta get up, go for a run."

"Yeah, it's time for my morning prayers," Adam said, sitting up on the bed.

"You're gonna get up this early to swim on your day off?" I asked incredulously.

He looked at me and grinned. "Absolutely." Then he looked back down to Simon. "You should take Wil running with you."

I barked out a laugh, making both men look at me. "Jesus, I haven't run since high school."

Adam climbed down to the foot of the bed, but before he climbed off, he slapped my ass. "Then it will do you good."

I scrubbed my hands over my face. "You two do this every day? Get up and go swimming and running?"

Adam waggled his eyebrows as he slipped on his shirt. "Helps build endurance, you know, stamina."

I groaned out a laugh.

Simon chuckled and got up, then picked his pants up off the table. "Put on some running gear and meet us at the stone steps in five."

I was going to have a heart attack, and Simon wasn't even out of breath. "How far do you normally run?" I asked.

"Up to the headland and back," he said, nodding off into the distance.

"Holy shit," I panted. "That's a long way." No wonder he was in such great shape.

Simon smirked. "You'll get a little farther each day."

"You mean I have to do this again?" I asked, like he'd lost his mind.

He laughed again. His dark hair and blue eyes shone in the sunrise. He really was a striking guy. I ran with him for a while but suggested he keep running without me, and I'd start running again on his way back. I slowed to a walk and watched him run effortlessly ahead of me, his body lithe and fluid.

It gave me time to catch my breath, but also time to think. When Simon had run up to the headland and made his way back, he slowed to a walk beside me. A sheen of sweat covered his bare torso, and his chest was heaving. But he asked me questions about my life in Alabama, about my work, and seemed interested in what I had to say. When we were at the steps of the hotel, Simon put his shirt back on, and we sat down and watched Adam swim. Our conversation soon turned to the man in the water.

I gave a pointed nod toward Adam. "He's a livewire."

Simon snorted. "And then some."

"Have you always sought out a third guy?"

Simon smiled at my question. "No, not always."

"It was his idea, though, wasn't it?" I asked.

"Why do you ask?"

"Because it seems Adam was the one who wanted it."

Simon chuckled. "Is that so? Do you get the impression I don't want it?"

I remembered just how much he'd wanted it last night, how hard he'd fucked and how hard he'd come. "Okay, well, not just him."

Simon chuckled, obviously remembering last night too. "After I checked you into your room, I told Adam you were here alone. He *did* ask me if I was interested in inviting you to join us," he admitted. "I think you know my answer."

The heat of embarrassment crept over my cheeks, and I nodded. "Oh."

"Is that wrong? That I told him you were here by yourself?"

I looked at Simon. His eyes were curious but equally serious. "No," I answered. "But you singled me out?"

"Hardly," he replied with a laugh. "You were already single, remember? I merely told Adam you were here alone, and when he saw you, he agreed."

I nodded, taking in this information. "Does it bother you?"

"What?"

"That he wants to bring other people into your bed?"

Simon shook his head. "No. Why would it?"

"Because you've never had a third guy around for this

long, right? Let alone for ten days." Then I added, "And because you're in love."

"And is love only for two people?" he retorted.

I thought about that for a moment. Despite the preconceived idea of what a relationship is—or should be—I could now see just how happy three people could be. "No, I guess it's not."

Simon smiled. "The only rules in love are the rules we set for ourselves. If Adam wants a third person in our bed, then that's fine with me."

"But you have to want it too."

Simon tilted his head, as if trying to understand something. "Why do you keep thinking I don't want this?"

I didn't answer. I couldn't. I didn't want him to admit he was only putting up with me for the sake of his boyfriend. And just then, we were interrupted by one of the kitchen staff.

"Excuse me, Simon?" the girl asked. "Got a sec?"

He looked at his watch. "Shit!" He got to his feet and walked with her into the building. I stood with a sigh and went back to my room.

And by the time Adam knocked on my door, I'd done some thinking. I knew he had two days off, and I knew it was very possible we'd spend those two days in bed. I let him in, and he grinned. "Ready for the best day ever?"

I smiled at him. It was impossible not to. "First, I think we need to set some rules."

Adam blinked. "Huh?"

I shook my head at his reaction. "Rules."

Ten minutes later, he'd dragged Simon into my room. "Can you please tell him? You tell him how I don't like rules."

Simon laughed and looked at me. "What rules?"

I took a deep breath and told Simon what I'd just told Adam. "I don't think we should have sex when it's not the three of us."

Adam looked at Simon and cried, "See? I told you it was ridiculous!"

Simon smiled at Adam, then looked at me. "Why?"

"I just thought it would be unfair to the person who's sitting out." Then I clarified, "But not me. You two can do what you want without me. I mean, you're a couple. I'm just the third wheel."

Adam put his hands on his hips. "You're not a fucking third wheel," he huffed, then he looked at Simon. "See?"

I laughed at Adam. He was like a kid who wasn't allowed candy.

"Look, Adam," I said gently, "what I mean is, you and I have two days together while Simon has to work. That's hardly fair to him. He'll be wondering what we're doing." Then I whispered, "And how we're doing it."

Adam looked at Simon and pouted. "Oh."

I walked up to him, standing closer so I could look in his eyes. "Just imagine if Simon had a day off while you had to work, and we spent it together, locked away in a bedroom, for hours and hours"—I groaned for effect —"and hours."

Adam frowned.

I cupped his face in my hands. "You wouldn't like that, would you? Wondering what we were doing without you?"

He shook his head slowly. "Not really."

"But we can kiss," I conceded. "And make out."

Adam looked suddenly hopeful. "Blow jobs?"

I snorted out a laugh and looked at Simon, who shrugged.

"Oh, thank God." Adam groaned, unbuttoning his

cargos. Sliding his hand under his briefs, he freed his semi-hard dick.

My mouth fell open in shock at his blatant suggestion. Simon laughed, then clicked his tongue. "Rules are rules. Blow jobs *are* allowed, Wil."

I looked at him, trying to gauge his reaction. "Are you sure you're okay with this?"

Simon smiled and nodded.

Adam looked at Simon and pumped his own cock. "Did you wanna watch?"

Simon looked at the time. "I've got about two minutes."

Adam grabbed my jaw with his free hand and pulled me in for a quick, hard kiss. "With this mouth, that won't be a problem."

I dropped to my knees. I took his beautiful cock in eagerly, sucking and licking for all my worth. Grunting and groaning, and with his hands around my jaw, he came down my throat. He didn't last the two minutes, not that I was counting.

And when I looked up, Simon was staring at me. He leaned down and kissed me, tasting Adam in my mouth. His eyes were dark and heavy-lidded, and he licked his lips. "I'm sure I could spare another two minutes."

I grinned and unzipped his pants.

CHAPTER FIVE

ADAM and I spent the day doing non-tourist things, as he called it. He took me to places only locals knew about and fed me lunch at one of his favorite cafés, where the woman behind the counter called him by name.

She looked like she'd been Photoshopped off a brochure for the Caribbean with her rich, dark skin, tight curly hair pulled back off her face, full lips, and colorful clothes. She looked me over as if not knowing whether to smile at me or not. Instead she asked Adam pointedly, "How's Simon?"

Adam slid his arm around my waist and pulled me close. "Simon's great, isn't he, Wil?" He looked at me and chuckled. "He was great last night. He was *great* this morning..."

I looked at the woman and could feel my cheeks heat with embarrassment. But she just shook her head and laughed. "I'm Dee, by the way," she said, smiling at me then.

I cleared my throat, swallowing my embarrassment. "Wilson Curtis."

"You boys grab a table. I'll be over to take your order," she said.

We took a seat and Dee followed us. Adam ordered us lunch and he chatted with Dee a little. She'd heard through the grapevine that Hartley was back, trying to get his hooks into anything and everything. When Dee left us to serve someone else, I asked Adam who this Hartley was.

"Developer," he answered.

Dee must have heard our conversation because from across the café, she added, "Good for nothing is what he is."

Adam nodded in agreement. "He used to be a local politician. He tried to stop the Keys from 'going to Hell' in the nineties," Adam said with a sad smile. "He ran an entire campaign to kick the gay community to the curb."

"But he lost, right?"

Adam nodded. "Yeah, he lost. So ever since, he's been buying up real estate, in particular gay hotels and gay clubs. He's trying to get rid of us one way or another."

"Sounds like he should move to my hometown."

Adam huffed out a laugh and nodded. Then he looked at me seriously. "Was it really that bad back home?"

I took a deep breath, then exhaled slowly. "Well, there certainly aren't gay hotels or gay clubs where I come from."

Adam shook his head. "Wait. What? Are you saying you've never been to a gay club?"

I bit my bottom lip and shook my head. I held in a snort. A gay club? In my home town? Hardly. "Ah, no."

A slow smile spread across his face. "Well, I know what we'll be doing tonight."

As we finished our meals, Adam tilted his head and looked at me. "Is this the first time you've been out with a guy in public?"

I finished my soda and nodded. "Not counting hanging out with the boys, yeah, I guess it is."

Adam shook his head in disbelief. "So when we walk out of here, if I held your hand, that'd be a first too?"

Held my hand? In public?

"Um..."

Adam shook his head again, stood up as he threw a twenty on the table, then held out his hand.

When I stared at him, completely uncertain, he just grinned like he always did. "Come on, Wil," he urged me. "After what we've done in your bed, the least you can do is hold my hand."

I snorted out a laugh. But then I took his hand in mine, and for the first time in my life, I walked out into the street, holding the hand of a man.

I don't know what I was expecting. Something. Comments from strangers, horrified looks, even verbal abuse.

But no one looked twice. No one cared.

Adam squeezed my hand, so I looked at him. He smiled at me, and I grinned from ear to ear.

It was a monumental step in my life. Such a simple act, one many couples took for granted, but the basic gesture of holding someone's hand for all the world to see was an epic milestone for me.

Adam laughed and shook his head. "You're so adorable." Then he squeezed my hand again. "If you think this is special, just wait till tonight."

It was still early by nightclub standards, but I was on my second drink and feeling a little braver. At first, the all-male, all-gay-male, all-hot-half-naked-gay-male clientele was over-whelming. I imagined I looked as wide-eyed and naïve as I felt. Adam fit right in and looked around as though he owned the place. He nodded to a few people and called some by name. He reassured me he wouldn't make me dance.

Yet.

He thought a few drinks would loosen me up a little. He was right.

I was buzzed. And horny.

Other guys, couples, started to dance, the music got louder, and the crowd got bigger. It was hospitality night, apparently, when the staff of local bars, hotels, and clubs got to play. Considering it was Tuesday night, but Adam's weekend, it made sense.

"What time did Simon say he'd get here?" I asked loudly, so Adam could hear me over the music.

He leaned right into me so I could feel his body heat. I could smell him. "As soon as he finishes up." His breath was hot in my ear. "Around ten-ish." He pulled back to check his watch. "Soon."

I nodded and, as much-needed distraction, sipped my drink, looking around at the other men.

"Why?" Adam asked with a sly grin. "Starting to regret the rules you made up?"

I chuckled at him and his blatant attempts at trying to get me to cave in. "You're not making it any easier."

And he hadn't been, either. But as much as he joked and made snarky comments about my rules of no sex without Simon, he respected it. Yes, he wanted sex, but he took my wishes seriously. He didn't want to abuse my trust any more than I wanted to abuse Simon's. He just liked to tease me about it.

Like earlier, after we'd had lunch, we'd gone back to the hotel and straight to my room. We'd lain on my bed and talked about anything and everything, and we'd made out a little. He was a sweet kisser with a magic tongue, and he tasted divine. I'd moaned, and he'd run his hand over the aching bulge in my pants but then he'd pulled away with a chuckle and a click of his tongue.

"Rules are rules," he'd said. And as he looked at me in the nightclub, he said those words again. Only this time he almost purred them.

I grinned at him, and with two beers worth of courage under my skin, I stepped right up close to him and put my free hand on his hip, pulling us together.

"Yes, rules are rules," I said, nudging my nose along his jaw. "But there were no rules about touching." I ran my hand around to his ass, squeezing it. "There were no rules about kissing," I whispered against the corner of his lips.

He grabbed the beer bottle out of my hand, and without another word, he dragged me out to the dance floor. And he grabbed me, hard. He smashed our hips together, one of his thighs between mine, and he ground into me. His eyes, dark and intense, never left mine.

The dance floor was a crowded sea of sweating, swaying men. I'd never danced before, not with a man. Not like this. Adam controlled me. We rocked, swayed. Danced.

Except it wasn't really dancing.

It was foreplay.

And I loved it.

The music, the movements, the moaning. All of it. It was intoxicating. It was arousing. It was like nothing else mattered.

Adam held my hips and my ass, and pressed his lips against my neck. I dug my fingers into his sides so I could grind my cock into his hip. I needed to *feel* him. I needed the friction.

Other men danced around us. The music changed a few times, song after song, and we never stopped. We kissed, licked, and nipped each other and I was hard, *achingly* hard. And all I could do was shamelessly rub myself against him. He didn't seem to mind. Not at all.

But then he turned me around and rubbed his cock against my ass. His hands crept under my shirt, hot on my skin, and his lips were behind my ear. His breaths were hot, wet and ragged.

"You're so hot," he panted. "All the men here want you."

I didn't bother opening my eyes. "They're looking at you."

Adam bit my neck and my whole body shuddered. I lifted my hands above my head, reaching back to pull his head closer, urging him, begging without words for him to do it again. And he did. His teeth scraped my skin and I moaned.

"Oh, Adam."

"Simon."

It took a moment for what he'd said to register in my lust-addled brain. My head fell forward and my eyes opened. "Huh?"

But right in front of us, like we were putting on a show just for him, was Simon.

He'd changed from his business pants and shirt. Now he was wearing jeans and a tight T-shirt the same color as his eyes. His eyes... his eyes were staring just above my shoulder, looking straight at Adam. And he licked his lips. I could feel Adam smile into my neck.

Simon took a step toward us, and I grabbed a fistful of his shirt, pulling him closer. "Oh thank God."

Simon chuckled. "Miss me?"

Adam's laughter resonated in my ear. "I think his rules of no sex without you are starting to wear him down."

I pulled Simon closer, his body now flush with mine. "No, the rule stays."

Simon leaned over my shoulder and kissed Adam. God, I loved it when they kissed with me in between them. But as soon as his lips had left Adam's, they found mine. Simon kissed me, deep and hard, while Adam rubbed against my ass.

A man beside us moaned, making Simon smile and break the kiss. Simon looked from me to Adam. "You two were putting on quite the show."

"Adam doesn't play fair," I told Simon. "He's been trying to coerce me all day."

Simon laughed, and Adam's chest vibrated as he chuckled. "He wouldn't give in though."

"Mmm," Simon hummed, rubbing his groin against mine, nuzzling his lips against my jaw. "I can feel how hard you are, Wil. You didn't want to *relieve* yourself?"

All I could do was shake my head. "Want both of you. It's better with both."

Adam reached up and, with a handful of my hair, pulled my head back, exposing my neck to Simon. As Simon attacked the newly exposed skin, Adam moaned in my ear. "It is better with both, isn't it? Two men fucking you at once. You like it, Wil, don't you?"

Adam's words, his hands, Simon's mouth, his hips. Their bodies. Their heat. "Oh, fuck. You're gonna make me come," I rasped.

Simon froze for just a second, then grabbed my hand and led us off the dance floor. I was about to question why, what, where, but he was on a mission. Simon had my hand and Adam had a hold of the back of my jeans as we jostled through the crowd. Finally Simon pushed through a door, leading us in.

To a bathroom.

There were other guys in there, but Simon didn't seem bothered. He walked us to the end stall, one I realized, once inside, was reserved for wheelchair access. We were no sooner through the entrance than the door was locked and Adam pushed me against the wall. Simon was beside Adam then, and both of them pushed against me, taking either side of my neck.

From the other side of the stall wall, I heard a chuckle and mumbled voices of the men who'd watched us walk in, and I didn't care.

I closed my eyes and just felt.

Two mouths, two tongues, four hands. They devoured me.

"Please," I begged. "Please."

With my eyes still closed, I could feel tugging on the fly of my jeans, then my aching cock was freed. I moaned at the relief, and I realized a little belatedly Adam's mouth was gone from my neck before it engulfed my dick.

My knees nearly gave out. I'm sure if Simon hadn't pressed me against the wall, I would have slid to the floor. I snaked one of my hands around Simon's neck. My other hand resting on Adam's head, fisting his hair. I groaned loudly, wantonly, as the pleasure became too much. Simon kissed me, hard, urgent, his tongue invaded my mouth while Adam's tongue twirled and teased my cock.

I couldn't have warned Adam if I'd tried. He must have

felt my body shake, because he pinned my hips to the wall behind me and swallowed me down.

I groaned into Simon's mouth as I came into Adam's. My body bucked and flexed as white-hot bliss ripped through me. Wave after wave of my orgasm left me boneless and spent. I slumped heavily onto Simon. His arms wrapped around me and held me up, and he smiled into my neck.

Adam was still licking me clean, and his eager tongue on my sensitive skin made me squirm. He stood up and without hesitation, he kissed Simon, letting him taste me.

I moaned. "Fuck."

They both turned to look at me. Although they both had hold of me, I fell back against the wall with a thump. All I could do was grin.

Adam chuckled and lifted my chin. "You in there, Wil?"

I barked out a laugh, and when I focused again, they were both smiling, with slightly swollen lips. "You're both so beautiful."

Simon looked at Adam. "You okay? Or do you need some relief too?"

Adam gave me a smug grin. "No, I'm good. I wanna wait till we get this boy back to his room. I think he could do with a good spit-roasting."

I'd seen enough porn to know what that meant, and they'd done it to me before. One cock in my ass, one down my throat. Simon and I both moaned in unison, and Adam chuckled at us. Simon kissed him soundly. "Love the way you think."

"I'm rather fond of it, too," I told them, earning a smile from Simon and a quick peck from Adam.

When I could stand unassisted, they stepped back,

giving me room to stand up straight and tuck myself back into my pants. While I made myself presentable, Adam asked Simon how work had gone.

"Ugh," Simon groaned and rolled his eyes.

Apparently Adam understood what that meant, or whom Simon was referring to, because he shook his head. "Why don't you two go out to the dance floor, and I'll get us drinks?" Adam asked rhetorically. He looked at Simon rather seriously. "You're not leaving until you're unwound and de-stressed."

Simon smiled fondly. "When I walked into the club and saw you two on the dance floor, believe me, work was the last thing I was thinking of." He opened the door.

To a little audience, apparently. They'd heard everything. They'd heard me moan, they'd heard me beg, and they'd heard me come.

One of them clapped.

My embarrassment crept hot up my neck and over my cheeks, and I ducked my head. Simon just smiled but didn't say anything, but Adam, well, Adam stopped and grinned. "Hello, gentlemen," he said. "Enjoy the show?"

"On the dance floor and in here," came one reply.

Oh God.

Simon pulled me toward the door, when someone jokingly called out, "Aren't you going to wash your hands?"

I turned to watch Adam deliberately lick his lips and tell them, "I didn't spill a drop." The audience of five or six men roared with laughter.

I was so mortified, my jaw almost hit the floor. I couldn't believe he'd said that. Simon just chuckled and dragged me by the hand out onto the dance floor.

When we'd ventured into the middle of the crowded room, Simon turned to face me. He slid his arm around me effortlessly, pulled me against him, and started to move.

"He has no shame," I said into his ear over the thumping music.

Simon laughed. "No, none. But he knows most of those guys." Then he pulled back to look at me, concerned. "Did what he said bother you?"

I shook it off. "No. I'm just not used to it, that's all."

Simon smiled, seeming happier knowing I wasn't upset. "How do you feel now?"

Remembering what we'd just done in the bathroom, I sighed happily. "Heavy and weightless all at the same time."

He chuckled in my ear. "So you're all right to stay for a little while longer?"

"I think I'll manage."

Simon smiled into my neck and kissed me there. "Good, because I could use a dance and a drink."

I slid my hands over his lower back, moving with him. "Don't drink too much or tire yourself out dancing," I teased him. "I hear there'll be a spit-roasting later."

Simon threw his head back and laughed, and he concentrated on making us dance. He was a better dancer than Adam, very fluid, very sensual, almost like how I'd imagined a classical dancer would move.

And I could tell he loved it.

Not necessarily dancing with me, just dancing. Moving, losing himself one song at a time. Not sexual, just letting go of his troubles.

I only needed to hold on for the ride.

Eventually, he led me off the dance floor over to where Adam was waiting with drinks. He'd been watching us, and he was smiling rather proudly by the time we got to him.

We talked for a while, telling Simon about our day,

though it was rather difficult over the music. I'd had three drinks, so I was feeling kind of buzzed, and after it was my turn to buy, I came back to find them dancing.

So I watched them.

They were slow-dancing, wrapped around each other, in their own little world.

They were truly beautiful. As individual men they were stand-outs, but together... well, together, they were something else entirely.

I looked on, waiting for jealousy to rear its ugly head—jealousy that they were in love without me, jealousy for what they had, for what they shared, jealousy because it wasn't me out there with one of them. Or with both of them.

But there was no jealousy.

None.

I felt... proud. I felt... *content* and *happy* as I watched them. There was no jealousy at all.

Though I wondered if I looked like that when I danced with either of them. I doubted I would've seemed that engrossed, that absorbed. Not like them. I wondered who on earth I could date back home that I would ever look so happy with.

No one.

And the odds of finding *two* men? Of having a three-way affair?

The likelihood of *that* made me snort.

"Something funny?" an unfamiliar voice beside me asked.

I turned to find a guy looking at me, obviously expecting me to answer him. He was okay-looking—tall, dark, and handsome, one might say. He had a nice smile.

"No," I answered him. "Just thinking." I turned to look back at the dance floor, back to Adam and Simon.

He put his drink down beside me and stood a little too close. "I saw you dancing earlier," he said smoothly. Then he gave a pointed nod toward the dance floor. "But it seems your dance partner has already found someone else."

I said, "Oh, well, he found him before me."

Confusion crossed his face, and he shook his head. Then he tried again. "I'm Deon," he said, offering me his hand. "That's one helluva Southern accent you have."

I shook his hand, not wanting to be rude. "Wilson. And I'm from Alabama."

"Well, Wilson from Alabama," he said with a grin. "Would you like to dance?"

"No, he wouldn't," a familiar voice said, making both our heads turn.

There stood Adam, with Simon behind him, looking at us. He was still smiling—he was always smiling—but it wasn't genuine.

"He's busy tonight," Adam went on to say, sliding his body right up next to mine and his arm around my waist. Then he looked at me with wide eyes. "Unless you wanted to go with him..."

I chuckled and looked at Deon. "Thank you for asking, but I am here with someone"—then I corrected—"with *them*. I'm here with *them*."

Adam planted a kiss on my lips. I handed Simon his drink, which earned me a peck on the lips, and when I looked back at Deon, he was staring at the three of us. He blinked slowly before a slow smile hinted at his lips. "So, three play in your game, yes?"

Simon answered flatly. "Yes."

"Can I interest you in a fourth?"

Jesus. Talk about a blunt proposition. I wasn't sure how I felt about bringing in another guy. I looked at Simon, waiting to see how he'd answer. Simon looked at me, then Adam, and finally back to Deon. He shook his head. "No, thanks. Three's the magic number."

Adam laughed and pulled Simon against the both of us, kissing the side of his neck. So I kissed down the other side of his neck, and I could feel the moan rumble in his throat. With Deon long forgotten, Adam moved to my neck, kissing and nipping, until he spoke in my ear. "God, we can't leave you alone for a minute, can we?"

I shook my head and tried to explain quickly. "I didn't... He approached me. I never..."

"He knows," Simon answered with a chuckle on behalf of Adam. "He's just toying with you."

"Oh."

Adam laughed again. "We'd better keep this country boy with us at all times, I think," he said, smiling at Simon.

I didn't want to draw attention to myself. I looked at them and bit my lip. "Am I doing something wrong?"

Adam grinned beautifully at me and shook his head. "You're so adorable," he said, and with his thumb he pulled my lip from between my teeth. "You did nothing wrong, Wil. Just your wide-eyed charm has guys going crazy for a taste, that's all."

I rolled my eyes, knowing damned well what he meant. "You mean crazy to take the naïve country boy home and fuck him stupid?"

Simon laughed and pecked my lips. "That too."

Adam smiled warmly. "Well, the position of taking said naïve country boy home and fucking him stupid has been filled, thank you very much."

I tried to smile at his joke, but then looked at them both. "Am I that naïve?"

Adam nodded cheerfully. "You've had countless guys trying to pick you up here and at the hotel, and you're still unaware."

I remembered the different guys chatting with me at the bar at the hotel, and I remembered Adam laughing at me when I hadn't even realized... I recalled the guys in the bathroom and now poor, dejected Deon.

"I'm just not used to it, that's all." I tried defending myself, but gave up. There wasn't much point. I *was* naïve when it came to guys—and gay clubs. I didn't have a fucking clue.

"Hey," Adam said, lifting my chin so I looked at him. "You're fucking adorable. You're sexy as hell and you don't even know it. So don't go being upset over anything."

Adam pulled me over to a stool at the table and pushed me onto it. Then he grabbed Simon and shoved him so he stood between my legs. "I'm going to the bar to get another round of drinks," Adam declared. He looked at Simon. "Keep him... *occupied* till I get back."

Adam disappeared into the crowd, and Simon just grinned. But he settled himself between my legs comfortably, leaning into me. I looked into his blue eyes.

"Adam keeps calling me adorable."

Simon nodded. "He likes you," Simon said easily, as if discussing the color of my shirt. He leaned in closer, nestling his groin into mine and pressing himself against me. He trailed his lips over my jaw. "But he's right."

I gripped his hips, keeping him right where he was. Having Simon with me like that was scrambling my brain. "Right about what?"

He kissed just below my ear. "You are adorable." Then

he ever-so-slowly licked my neck. "And you are sexy as hell."

I shivered and pulled his hips closer into mine. I could feel his semi-hard cock. Mine twitched as it stirred back to life. He planted open-mouthed kisses over my neck. When he scraped his teeth across my skin, I shivered and he chuckled.

Adam returned with drinks and seemed a little pleased at just how Simon had kept me *occupied*. Simon stopped kissing my neck and talked with Adam, though he never moved from between my thighs. Adam stood on the outside of my thigh in the perfect position for me to kiss either man's neck and jaw while they talked.

They sipped their drinks and talked over the music, about work and staff problems and other people I didn't know, while I finished my drink and took turns at lavishing kisses on all the exposed skin I could. I opened my legs wider and pulled Simon in closer, keeping one hand on his lower back and the other hand on Adam's.

And while I scraped my teeth over Simon's neck like he'd done to me, I ran my hand over his ass and down the back of his thigh. His head fell back and he groaned. He stood back from me but took my hand, pulling me off the stool and toward the dance floor. I managed to grab Adam's arm and brought him with us. I didn't want anyone sitting out this time.

Halfway across the crowded dance floor, Simon turned and cupped both hands around my jaw, and he kissed me. Hard.

His desire, his want, surprised me. But I sure as hell didn't object.

I opened my mouth for him, allowing him complete

access. I could taste him and the Scotch he'd not long finished. But mostly him. *Oh, Simon.*

And Adam was behind me, kissing my neck, rubbing himself against my ass. His hands were on my chest and moved over my stomach before his fingers slid under the waistband of my jeans. And when his hands weren't on me, they were on Simon, pulling the three of us together. When I needed to breathe, Simon would kiss Adam, and before too long, we were a panting, writhing mess.

God, it felt so good.

I couldn't help but arch into both of them. I wanted both of them. So fucking much. I ached to have them. And with four drinks and raw lust holding my inhibitions hostage, I told them they should take me home and fuck me. I *needed* both of them—one in my ass, one down my throat. Any way they wanted to, they could have me, however they wanted, as many times as they needed.

And so, God help me, that's exactly what they did.

CHAPTER SIX

I WOKE UP EARLY. The sun had barely shown any interest in rising. Adam was next to me, in the middle, and Simon was on the other side, both still sound asleep. By the time we'd actually got to sleep, I'd been exhausted, thoroughly sated, and I'd slept like a log.

I lay there and stretched out slowly, ironing out the kinks, feeling every inch of my body. I'd been fucked, used, and fucked again. I felt achy and sore.

I felt like a million dollars.

Rolling onto my side, I looked over at the two men in bed with me. Adam was on his back and seemed to be smiling even in his sleep. Simon was on his side, facing us. His long, dark eyelashes fanned across his cheeks. His lips were slightly open, and he snored softly.

Both men were stark contrasts of the other, not just in looks but in personality. Adam was the blond-haired, happy, surfer-looking guy, whereas Simon was the dark-haired, serious businessman. Both men were undeniably beautiful.

I tried not to think about where I fit in with them. Me, with my ordinary brown hair and ordinary looks, living a closeted life, compared to these two very out-and-proud guys. I wouldn't let myself overthink things like how my time here was limited, how I knew at some point I'd be saying goodbye or how I had to go back to my non-life in Alabama.

It was only fun and sex with them. I knew that. That was what I'd openly agreed to. And I would never regret it, not ever. In fact, my time here had been the absolute highlight of my sexual adult life.

I was getting a handle on just who I was supposed to be. The *man* I was supposed to be.

This man, who'd spent years hiding, lying and denying, was in bed with two other men after a night of drinks and dancing, the happiest he'd ever been.

The same man who had a house, a broken business, and a town of homophobic, small-minded assholes waiting for him to return.

That was something I didn't want to think about.

Needing to pee but not wanting to wake the others, I rolled out of bed. Stifling a groan at the dull ache in my backside, I stood up and gingerly made my way to the bathroom. After I'd relieved my bladder, washed my face, and brushed my teeth, I snuck back into bed.

I'd settled back down when Simon's voice croaked, "You feel okay?"

I leaned up to look at him and smiled. "Yeah, I feel fine."

"Not sore?" he asked. "You sounded like it hurt to move."

Adam chuckled. He didn't even open his eyes. "Not surprising," he mumbled. "What we did to him."

I tweaked his nipple, making him squirm. "You certainly weren't complaining."

He chuckled again, slowly opening his eyes to look at me. "Hell, no. Last night was—" He stopped talking so he could yawn, then he stretched out like a cat in the sun. "Mm, last night was *so* good." He slid his hand down to give his morning wood a squeeze.

Simon chuckled.

Ignoring Adam, I looked at Simon. "Is he always so insatiable?"

Simon rolled onto his back. "Always."

Grinning, Adam rolled into me, snuggling and wriggling, with one arm heavy on my waist. "Mm, minty," he mumbled into my neck.

I wrapped my arm around him. "Toothpaste," I said in explanation. I leaned up on my bent arm to get a better look at Simon. He was looking back at us, smiling to himself as he watched his boyfriend snuggle with another man. When his eyes met mine, I asked him, "What time do you work till tonight?"

"Actually"—he hesitated—"I have today off."

Adam quickly turned in my arms to look at him. "You do?"

Simon nodded. "I have to work tonight, from five till close, but I'm free all day."

Adam literally cheered. "Yay!" And leaving my arms, he quickly rolled over to snuggle into Simon. It made us laugh.

Figuring they didn't have time off together very often, I offered them my absence. "So what are you two going to do with a day off together?"

Adam looked at me, confused. Simon's eyes darted to mine, and his smile died. Simon frowned. "Well, I was thinking we could go to the Fort Zachary Taylor beach, spend the day there, and have lunch."

"The three of us?" Adam asked, though it was more of a statement than a question.

"Well, yeah," Simon said, unsure. Then he looked at me and said, "If that's okay with you?"

"Of course it is!" I said quickly.

Shit. Simon was so hard to read. He seemed so aloof with me sometimes, silently reminding me that this threesome was Adam's idea and he was just along for the sex. Then other times, he seemed to genuinely like me.

I looked at both of them. "I just didn't want to intrude on your personal time, that's all," I clarified, not wanting to offend Simon or Adam. "I didn't want you to feel obligated to include me if you'd prefer some alone time. Because I'd understand if you do..." God, I was rambling.

Adam rolled over, snuggling his back into Simon, but now facing me. "Wil, please stop talking," he said to me with a smile. "You're not intruding. We're not obligated. If we didn't want to include you, we wouldn't."

Simon looked at me, appearing both puzzled and amused, and I felt the need to apologize to him. "I'm sorry. I didn't mean to imply anything. I kind of ruined it, didn't I?"

He surprised me by laughing. "Don't worry about it."

Adam sighed loudly. "Well, it's time I got up and went to church." Then he turned to Simon. "I won't be long. Don't want to cut into any of your time off."

Simon smiled. "Take as long as you want. We can head over when you're done and have lunch. How does that sound?" he asked, looking at Adam, then at me.

"Perfect," Adam said.

I nodded, because in all honesty, it did sound like a perfect way to spend the day.

Simon smiled. "Well, you"—he playfully smacked Adam's ass—"should get going, or the tide will start without you." Adam rolled his eyes and chuckled, but he did get up. Then Simon looked at me, a little uncertain. He asked, "Did you want to come running again?"

"Sure," I answered promptly, not wanting to upset him or offend him further. Then remembering the dull sting in my backside, I added, "Though I'm sure my ass won't agree."

Adam, now half-dressed, barked out a laugh and walked over to goose my butt cheek. "Does your ass need a day off?" he said with the devil's grin.

"Yes," I said with a laugh, swatting his hand away. "But that's okay. Simon and I can take turns fucking you instead."

Adam stood up straight, clearly visualizing the very thought in his mind. He groaned and started to unbutton the jeans he'd just put on. "Mm, sounds good to me," he murmured.

Simon laughed but got out of bed and put his hands on Adam to stop him. "Water. Swim. Now," he ordered, turning Adam around and pushing him toward the door. Then he looked at me. "You can't say stuff like that to him, or we'll never leave."

I laughed, and as Simon threw on his jeans and pushed Adam out the door with him, he smiled at me. "See you on the beach in five."

———

We ran the stretch of sand near the shoreline up toward the headland. It was an amicable silence, friendly. And if Simon felt at all uncomfortable, he hid it well.

I know I'd apologized before, but I wanted to clear the air. "I'm sorry about before. I think it's great you've taken the day off."

He looked at me as he ran beside me. "Stop apologizing. Do you always try and make everyone else happy?"

I knew damn well I did. My silence was answer enough.

"When are you going to start doing things that make you happy?"

"I am. Now," I said, trying to steady my breathing. "I'm spending two weeks with two gorgeous men. That makes me happy."

Simon slowed his run to a walk, more for my benefit than his, I'm sure. "So when I mentioned taking the day off, you presumed you weren't invited?"

"Well..." I puffed, putting my hands on my hips, taking in deep breaths. "You and Adam are a couple..."

"Well, technically, yes. But while you're here, we're not."

I looked at him, confused. "What?"

"When there are three men in that bed, there are three opinions, three minds. Three sets of feelings. No one should sit on the outside, isn't that what you said?"

I nodded. "Something like that."

"It's a good philosophy," he said with a nod, looking toward the headland. "It was... thoughtful."

I smiled at him and his open acknowledgement of—and unspoken thanks at—the rules I'd imposed. "Come on," I said, nodding toward the headland and started off jogging again.

Simon caught up easily, and when I'd had enough, he kept on his usual run while I walked it out. Surprisingly, my ass wasn't too sore, and even more surprisingly, I found myself not overthinking anything.

I just enjoyed the early morning sun, the sound of the ocean, and the smell of the salt water. There were other walkers, joggers, and people with dogs. It was peaceful.

I must have lost track of time, because all of a sudden Simon ran up beside me, slapped me on the ass with a laugh, and kept running. This time I caught up to him, and by the time we'd made it back to the hotel, we were both puffing.

Instead of heading up the stone steps toward the hotel, Simon stopped on the sand and pulled off his shoes and socks. "Swim before breakfast," he said as he peeled off his T-shirt. He took off toward the water. "What are you waiting for?"

I shook my head, and with a grin, I left my shoes, socks, and shirt next to Simon's and followed him in.

The water was cool, to put it mildly, and Simon and I swam, ducking under the surface and swimming around each other in a comfortable silence. By the time we came in for breakfast, I was starving but feeling energized and refreshed and had no doubt in my mind I'd be in need of an afternoon nap.

All this eating healthy and exercising was going to kill me.

We were having breakfast in the open seating area, enjoying the morning sun after our swim, when an employee interrupted. There were issues with one staff member, a guy named Mikel, or Michel, or something else starting with an M, and it was obvious this was not the first time. At first Simon said he'd deal with it later, but it must have gotten the better of him, because with gritted teeth he stood and stalked off into the kitchen.

"Isn't he supposed to be having a morning off?" I asked.

Adam sighed. "Miguel makes Simon's job twice as stressful. He's a prick with an attitude."

"Hmm," I hummed. "Sounds like Simon could use a stress-reliever before we leave."

A slow grin spread across Adam's face and his eyes flickered with mischief. "Wil, I do believe I like the way you think."

So that was what we did. Simon came back to the table, jaw clenched and quietly seething, so we took him into my room. Within seconds, Simon's shorts were around his ankles, and while Adam fell to his knees and sucked him, hard and fast, I knelt behind Simon and spread his ass cheeks before running my tongue along his most sensitive flesh.

In all the sexual positions we'd tried—and there had been a few—Simon had never bottomed. As far as I knew, he'd never been breached that way. Well, not in my presence anyway. He tensed a little when he realized where I was, what I was doing, but as I tongued his hole, he leaned his hands on the wall above Adam's head, giving me better access, and he moaned like I'd never heard him moan.

I flicked my tongue harder while Adam worked his mouth over Simon's cock, and by the way he trembled and whined, I knew he wouldn't last long. Adam grunted, so I pushed my tongue into Simon's ass, hard and deep, and Simon bucked and groaned as he came.

His whole body shook as he slumped against the wall, trying to catch his breath. "Jesus."

Adam chuckled, and bending around Simon's legs, he

leaned forward, holding my face for a kiss that tasted of pure Simon. I might have moaned.

Simon murmured from above our heads, "Fuck, you two are so hot."

Adam and I smiled as we kissed, but our mouths never stopped moving, and soon Simon had one hand on my head and his other hand on Adam's. With a fistful of our hair, he pulled our mouths apart, only to lean down and join his mouth to ours.

With open lips, our tongues tangled, the three of us kissed.

Adam hummed. "Wil thought you might need a stress-reliever before we went anywhere today."

Simon looked into my eyes, and he smiled before he kissed me. "Thank you."

"Feeling less stressed?"

"Hell, yes," Simon said with a laugh. He kissed me again, then Adam.

Seeing Simon outside of work, even if it was just for a few hours, was great. Dressed in board shorts, a plain T-shirt, flip-flops, and sunglasses, instead of his usual uniform, he was a picture of relaxation. It was a little different from before we'd left the hotel, that was for sure.

And he was relaxed. As we walked along the beach, as we snorkeled, and finally as we lounged in the beach chairs in the shade, he was like a different guy. Well, not different per se. It was just good to see him being himself. He threw his head back and laughed. He was carefree and, well, less stressed. It was easy to see why he and Adam were a couple, the way they laughed together, looked at each other.

I looked at them from my beach chair. Adam was in the middle of us. "Do you guys get to do this often?" I asked them.

"Not as often as we'd like, but yeah," Adam answered. "Once every couple of weeks we find a way to get away."

Simon looked out toward the flat, blue water. "You know what it's like when you run a business. Free time isn't exactly free."

I nodded, thinking back to my restaurant back home because I knew exactly what he meant. And right on cue, my cell phone rang. I looked at the number. "And speak of the devil," I mumbled before answering. "Callie!"

"Hey, Mister Man of Leisure," she goaded me. "How's the Florida sun?"

The sound of her voice made me happy. "Good, Cal. How're things going up there? Everything under control?"

I rolled off my chair and walked off a few yards, giving a bit of courteous distance between me talking on the phone and Adam and Simon.

Callie chatted brightly, telling me all about what I'd been missing at home, which admittedly wasn't much. People were still talking about me—the scandalous rumors were still buzzing along the grapevine. Callie tried to laugh it off when she told me, but it still stung.

"But they're coming into the restaurant again? You've been busy..."

"Yeah," she said quietly, and I understood. She didn't have to explain.

"They're happy to eat there as long as the chef's not gay."

Her silence was my answer. *Fuck.*

"They won't let it go, will they?" I asked her.

"Sure they will," she said. "Just give them time."

"How much time?" I asked. "Until I'm broke?"

Callie sighed and changed the subject. She'd been out to check on my house, making sure it was as I'd left it. As she talked, I turned back to look at Adam and Simon, some thirty yards away, on the chairs in the shade. They were talking and smiling. Just looking at them made me smile.

"Wil?" Callie's voice snapped me back.

"Yeah? Sorry..."

"I asked if you were still spending time with that other guy?" she repeated. "Or did you meet someone else?"

My grin widened. "Maybe."

I heard her gasp through the phone. "Who is he? Is he cute?"

I laughed. "Um... well..."

"Wilson Curtis, you better not leave me hanging."

I chuckled at Callie. I knew when she called me by my full name, she meant business. And with the safety net of telling her over the phone, I took a deep breath and added, "Well, it's not really a *he*. It's more like a *they*..."

She was silent, obviously trying to make sense of what I said. "What?"

"Well, it is a *he*," I clarified. "But it's not one *he*..." Then I added, "It's *two*."

"Two?" Callie gasped again. Then she drawled out, "Wilson Curtis, you sly dog." I could hear the smile in her voice.

"I know!" I laughed at the ridiculousness of it all. "They're great though, Cal. Adam's the fun one, and Simon's the serious one of them."

"Jeez. Wil, you make it sound like these two guys are a couple."

I knew she'd presumed when I said *two* that I'd meant I'd scored twice with two separate men. "Um," I started, unsure how to explain. "Well, they are a couple."

Callie was quiet again, trying to get the scenario right in her head. "So they're a legit couple, as in boyfriends?"

"Yes."

"Then what are you to them?"

I changed the phone to my other ear and gave a quick glance back to the two men in question. They were still talking. "Dunno, Cal. I haven't really asked them that," I answered honestly. "Just a bit of fun, I guess. It doesn't matter. I turned up here alone, and they're taking it upon themselves to make sure I have the best time."

"So they're using you while you're there to fulfill some fantasy?"

"I don't know, Callie," I replied, my tone rather short. "Maybe it's mutual."

She huffed into the phone. "I'm not criticizing or judging, Wil. I just worry, that's all."

I exhaled through puffed cheeks. "I know, Cal." And I did know. She was my best friend. She'd been with me through everything. "I know you worry."

"Just tell me you're being safe and I'll leave it alone."

"Of course I am."

"Good," she sighed, sounding relieved. "That's good." Then she sighed again. "You can still give me details when you get home."

I laughed into the phone. "Not sure you want *all* the details, Cal."

She laughed. "Yeah, well, okay. Not all the details."

My smile faded. One week. Just over a week. One week, and my time here would be done. My time with Adam and Simon would be done. It made my stomach twist.

"You okay, Wil? You've gone quiet on me." She knew me so well.

I couldn't contain the desperation in my voice. "Callie, it's so good here. It's so free. I walked down the street holding his hand, Cal. In public! Do you have any idea what that's like? For the first time in my life..."

"Oh, Wil..." she breathed into the phone.

"Fuck, Callie."

"Then make the most of what time you have left," she replied. "Make it the best week of your life."

I scrubbed my hand over my face, and when I looked at Adam and Simon, they were both looking at me. "It's already been the best week of my life, Cal."

Callie was silent for a long moment. Then she said, "Wil, Rod asked about you. He wanted to know if I'd spoken to you."

I heard what she said. I heard the words. But in that moment, I understood something very clearly. "Callie, you know what? I don't want to know. I don't care."

"Wil?"

"Yeah?"

"I'm glad to hear it. He's an ass, and you deserve better."

I snorted. She never had liked him. Before I could say anything else, she said, "Right. I have a restaurant to run, and you have some fun to be had. Now quit wasting time talking to me and go find your man."

I laughed. "Um, Cal, I just told you. It's not one man. It's two."

I swear I could hear her roll her eyes. "Then go find your... men."

The line clicked dead, and I grinned. *My men.* I liked the sound of that.

I walked back to where they were and all but fell onto my chair. "Sorry about that."

"Everything okay?" Adam asked.

I nodded, not wanting to divulge my home life troubles and put a damper on the day. "Callie's got it all under control. She's been out to my house, checked on a few things."

"Oh," Simon said. "Everything okay?" he repeated Adam's question but then added, "Your house okay?"

"Yeah." I nodded, though I don't think either of them were convinced.

"Do you own your own house?" Adam asked.

I nodded. "It was my parents' house. They died two years ago, so I kind of inherited it."

"Oh," Simon said. "I'm sorry."

"Yeah, I'm sorry," Adam agreed. He shook his head and frowned. "I didn't know."

"'S'okay," I told them. "You couldn't have known."

"Have you got any brothers or sisters?" Simon asked. This was the first real personal information we'd exchanged, which was odd, considering how very personal we'd been.

"No," I answered. "None. Have you?"

Simon nodded. "One brother, one sister. Still got both parents and they're still married."

I looked at Adam. "Family?"

He shook his head and answered quietly, "None."

Simon was quick to jump in, moving the conversation along, and I deduced just as quickly Adam's family issues were not something he was comfortable discussing.

Adam sat up and seemed to have had enough of this conversation. He peeled off his shirt. "I'm going for a swim. Who's with me?"

Silly question, really. We both were, of course.

On the way back to the hotel, Simon made some phone calls, including one to the café where Dee worked. We stopped in on our way and were greeted by Dee herself with warm hellos and a huge grin. Simon and Dee caught up, apparently quite close friends, and I understood her coldness toward me when she'd thought Adam was now with me.

Talk turned to that Hartley developer guy, and Dee shook her head, suddenly fuming. I still didn't really know what was going on, but from what I could understand, someone had sold out to Hartley. He'd secured ownership of one gay bar, apparently. "I'll call you and tell you all about it," she told Simon. "But he's turning Key West straight, one development at a time."

Dee got busy with other customers and we sat at a booth, Adam and Simon on one side, me on the other, facing them. They sat close together, their sides touching, and Simon had one arm around Adam's waist. It was sweet.

I loved seeing them so wrapped up in each other, so very happy. It truly was a pleasure to witness.

Our sodas were delivered, and Simon held up his drink and said, "To a great day."

I clinked my glass to his, then Adam's, and Adam did the same. Only when he tapped his drink against Simon's, he looked at him and spoke just for him. "I love you."

And my stomach clenched. My heart rate took off.

Simon grinned at him and returned the sentiment. "Love you, too."

It was the first time I'd heard those words uttered between them. I wasn't surprised, not at all. Anyone could see they were in love... but to hear it...

I looked down at the table between us, wanting to give them their moment. I wondered why my heart thumped funny, why hearing those words, those very special three little words, made my heart rate spike, why my stomach was in knots.

It wasn't jealousy.

It wasn't jealousy at all.

It was longing.

I tried to squash the feeling. I tried to tamp down the yearning in my belly for what they had. And I tried to ease the aching realization that what I'd thought was love, what I'd had with Rod, hadn't been love at all.

It hadn't even been close.

"Wil, you okay?" Simon's voice startled me.

"Yeah," I answered with a smile. "It's all good."

Neither looked convinced. Adam tilted his head. "Sure everything's okay back home?"

I shrugged. "As good as it's gonna get."

"Wanna talk about it?" Simon asked.

"Not really," I said.

Dee came to our table with her arms full of food. I was grateful for the distraction, and the morning's activities had given me quite an appetite. I started to eat, and when I looked back up at them, Adam was looking at me, his food untouched.

Simon looked at Adam. "You know what?" he asked, trying to lighten the mood. "It seems Wil needs some *de-stressing* too."

Mental images of how we'd de-stressed Simon earlier today flashed through my mind, and I almost choked on some salad.

Adam chuckled, then his smile died and his brow pinched. "But you were both going to take turns fucking me! Wil said so!" He looked genuinely put out but then tried not to smile. "You can't promise that kind of fun and not deliver."

I chuckled, a dozen shades of embarrassed, while Simon just laughed cheerfully. He patted Adam's hand. "Oh, we'll deliver. Don't you worry about that."

CHAPTER SEVEN

DELIVER WE DID. We took turns fucking Adam all right, but not one at a time. We did it together. Simon and I both prepped him, licking, sucking, and fingering him, stretching him.

Adam was on all fours on the bed, while Simon and I knelt beside him, behind him. Simon slid into him first, slowly, deliciously.

And I watched.

I watched Simon's long cock slide in, then pull almost all the way out and push back in. Again and again.

"Oh, baby," Simon whispered.

Adam moaned in response. "Fuck, you feel so good."

Simon groaned, almost painfully. So I kissed him. Fucking hard. I held his face and thrust my tongue into his mouth until we needed air.

Then he pulled out of Adam, his cock still hard as steel. He looked at me. "Your turn," he said gruffly. "Fuck him like you mean it."

I pumped my cock in my fist once, making sure the

condom was rolled all the way down and nicely slicked with lube, and I slid straight in.

Adam was still tight, and oh-so-hot, and I pushed in as deep as I could. Adam arched his back. "Oh, fuck! Wil! Yeah, baby, just like that!"

Simon moved to Adam's side and using a handful of hair, he pulled his head back. Leaning down, Simon smashed his mouth over Adam's. I could see their moving tongues, thrusting in time with my cock in his ass.

He felt so good. So, so fucking good.

Simon now knelt in front of Adam, lifting him to a kneeling position, while I was still buried in his ass. He cupped his face adoringly, lovingly, and whispered, "You know how beautiful you are right now?"

Adam moaned.

"With Wil's cock in your ass, you know how good you look?"

This time Adam and I groaned together. My thrusts were losing rhythm. I wasn't going to last long.

"You like him inside you, don't you?" Simon's voice was husky, low. "He fills you up so good."

Simon's words, his voice, his face, Adam's body, his moans... God, I was so on edge, so close, but I didn't want to come. Not yet.

I pulled out slowly, reluctantly, and my cock ached in protest. "Simon?"

Simon was quickly beside me, easing back into Adam. They both groaned, and Adam's body started to writhe. "Oh, Sy. God, yes."

Simon slammed into him, harder, harder. His fingers dug into his hips as he pounded into him.

All I could do was watch.

And pump and squeeze myself, trying to ease the ache, the throbbing need.

"Can't hold it," Simon grunted, then bucked one final time and stilled over Adam. His body was taut, his muscles stretched tight, and his head fell back as he came.

Simon groaned and slid out of Adam. "Finish him, Wil," he mumbled, before lying down next to Adam, kissing him, while I took my place behind him. I lifted his hips, pushed down on his back, and slid my cock back into him.

He lifted his mouth from Simon's only to groan as I plowed into him. Simon put his hands to Adam's face and pulled Adam's mouth back to his, kissing with open lips and sliding tongues. I sank every inch of me into Adam, rolling my hips and grinding deeper, making him whine and groan.

I pressed against his gland, making him buck.

"Oh, Wil! Right there! Yes, please. Again!"

I did as he'd asked, over and over, until he screamed into Simon's mouth. His ass clenched around me, and I was done. I couldn't fight it anymore.

I didn't want to.

Adam's cock spurted in thick bursts onto the bed beneath us, and I swelled inside him, pleasure ripping through me, pulsing hot and thick into the condom. We collapsed in a sweaty, sticky, sated mess of limbs and ragged breaths.

"Fuck."

"Yeah."

Adam chuckled. "Yeah."

The next day officially marked the one-week-to-go on my vacation calendar.

Seven days.

Then six.

Then five.

Adam and Simon had been great. Better than great. Perfect, really. They had to work, of course, but I ran with Simon in the morning, then he'd join me for coffee while we ate breakfast. Adam would join us after his swim, always smiling, outwardly happy that Simon and I seemed to get along.

And we did. Conversations with Simon were usually more professional—business, sales percentages, marketing. It was hard to tell if he was avoiding personal questions or if he enjoyed having someone to talk shop with.

Conversations with Adam were usually fun and flirty. That wasn't to say he couldn't have sensible, intelligent conversations, just that we usually ended up laughing and talking crap. He asked me never-ending questions about my ex, Rod, and best friend, Callie, about other friends, and about my hometown. He avoided asking questions about my family, I presumed, so I wouldn't ask about his.

And that was okay. If he didn't want to talk about it, I certainly wasn't about to push him.

But the discussions between us as a whole were becoming more personal. So was the sex. Maybe it was my imagination, maybe it was me wishing, but it seemed to me the touches got softer, the kisses got sweeter. More intimate. It was still hot—damn hot. The different ways three men could fuck seemed endless. Simon usually orchestrated what we did in bed, and he was rather... inventive.

They spent every night in my bed, the three of us wrapped around each other. Waking with the sun, we'd run while Adam swam, we'd have breakfast, they'd go to work, and I'd spend the day doing not much at all.

Like I said. Perfect.

But on Saturday, my fourth to last day there, an hour before the lunch shift started, Simon was taking a ten-minute break and had joined me at a table overlooking the water when one of the kitchen staff walked out. She was a slim, redheaded woman, about ten years older than us. She seemed peeved.

"Simon?"

"Yes, Sydney?"

"Can I have a word?"

Simon gave a loud sigh. "Yes," he said, his patience clearly worn thin. He made no move to stand or leave, indicating to her she could speak in front of me. "What is it?"

Sydney looked at me, then to Simon. "Um, the seafood delivery never came."

Simon gritted his teeth. "You called them?"

"Yeah, I did." Then she grimaced and said, "Miguel never placed the order."

Simon looked at his wristwatch. "Fuck!" He stood abruptly, mumbled an apology to me, then walked with Sydney back into the kitchen.

I felt sorry for Simon because he had to deal with disrespectful and inconsiderate staff, but I could tell from the anger rolling off Simon that this Miguel would bear the brunt of it.

I didn't want to see that.

I figured the kitchen staff, namely Sydney, was in for a less-than-pleasant lunch shift. It was a Saturday and if last week was anything to go by, new clients would be arriving for their weekend stay and things would start to get busy.

I stood and followed them into the kitchen, into an area that, as a guest, I was probably not supposed to go.

"Need a hand?"

Simon stuck his head out from the cool storeroom, obviously a little more than surprised to see me. "Wil, what are you doing?"

"Offering my help."

"No," he said flatly. Then as an afterthought, he added, "Thank you, but no."

I looked to Sydney and another staff member, who were both regarding us, and when they looked behind me, I turned to find Adam. He must have followed me in.

"Look, Simon," I started. "You need another set of hands. And you have them. Me, sitting there staring at the ocean." I held up my hands. "A pair of fully qualified chef hands doing nothing."

Simon shook his head. "Wil, you're a guest here. I couldn't ask you to do that."

"You didn't ask. I offered." I looked then at Adam, who was watching us like a tennis match. He seemed a little apprehensive, like this could go either way. I looked back at Simon. "I could go to the fish market, but I don't know my way around. You can't go because you're expecting the weekend's bookings to arrive." Everyone was staring at me, and I figured it was all or nothing. Simon hadn't even blinked. "And I assume Sydney has prep to do before lunch starts?"

Sydney nodded. "Produce, mainly. I need to work on salads and steam the vegetables. And I'll need to start the sauces." She looked at me apologetically. "They're normally done by now."

Easy. I shrugged. Looking at Sydney—and deliberately *not* looking at Simon—I asked her, "If you left now to go to the seafood markets, would you be back by the time lunch starts?"

She looked at the clock on the wall, then looked at me. "Should be."

I looked at Simon. "Strictly prep work, no cooking, no service."

He sighed, resigned. "Wil..."

I smiled at him, knowing I'd won this one, and walked to the sink to wash my hands. When I turned back to them, Simon's expression hadn't changed, but Adam was now grinning. I turned back to soaping my hands to hide my smile.

Sydney pulled off her apron, grabbed her keys and she stopped. She pointed to different shelves. "Boards, trays, knives..."

"Go," I told her. "I've eaten here enough to know how you want it done."

She waved, then disappeared. I could hear the waitstaff banging around in the storeroom, which left me alone in the kitchen with Simon and Adam. I dried my hands and stepped around Simon, quickly grabbing the large bag of carrots from the walk-in refrigerator. He was still staring at me when I found the chopping board, peeler, and knife.

I smiled at him. "If you're just gonna stand there, you can help me."

Adam chuckled and Simon made a huffing sound, his glare softening somewhat. "I don't know whether to be *really* grateful or *really* pissed off at you."

I looked over my shoulder, making sure we were still alone. I turned back to Simon. "You can thank me later."

Adam laughed this time and pulled on Simon's arm. "Leave him, Sy. He's got work to do."

And I did. And I enjoyed it, this normally mundane

task of prep work—chopping, dicing, julienning this, slicing that. I'd taken enough notice of what I'd been served over the last week to know procedure and plating, so that was what I did. I prepared single-serve salads in separate bowls, steamed carrots with a drizzle of honey, steamed beans with sesame seeds, creamy mashed potatoes, and I even made the tomato and green pepper salsa.

I guessed at the dressings, and on tasting, I got it pretty close. The jus was on simmer, reducing nicely, and I was cleaning down my work station when Sydney got back fifty minutes later.

She slid the large Styrofoam box on the counter.

"Jeez," she said, looking around at what I'd done. "Over-achiever, much?"

I laughed. "Don't tell Simon."

Sydney snorted. "What, that you're good with your hands? I think he already knows that."

My mouth fell open, and I could feel myself blush. Sydney just laughed. "Oh, come on," she said. "Don't be shy now. I've seen how they are with you."

She's seen how they are with me? I glanced at her. "What do you mean?"

She opened the box, pulled out some fish, and rolled her eyes. "Simon and Adam."

I shook my head in full denial mode. "I don't know what you're talking about."

Sydney put the whole fish in a tray and pushed the tray away. She looked at me. "You don't need to deny anything here, sugar."

My mouth opened and closed a few times while my brain scrambled for something to say. *Shit, shit, shit.* I didn't know what to say. She was openly acknowledging my sexuality, and I was stuck for words. The tray of fish slid in front of me.

"Can you fillet fish?"

I nodded and swallowed thickly. "Sure."

So we stood side by side, filleting fish, and Sydney talked. I learned she did mostly breakfast and lunch shifts and any other shift Miguel wouldn't. She'd been working there for three or so years, and she really didn't seem to care that I'd all but admitted I was gay. Well, my inability to say anything otherwise had probably given me away anyway.

She knew, and she didn't care.

Even though she worked at a gay hotel, it still stunned me that I could come out to someone so freely.

We could see the dining area start to fill up, and when the first order came in, I covered and put the last of the fish in the cool room and left Sydney to it.

Both Adam and Simon were busy, so I left them to it too. I was in need of a shower to rid myself of the lingering fishy smell but opted to change straight into my swimming gear and hit the water instead.

I swam, then walked the beach until I was hot, then I swam again. When I'd had enough, I headed back to my room and showered. When I was respectable—and had plucked up enough courage to face Simon—I headed to the bar.

Adam was cleaning up and he grinned at me as though I was an old friend he hadn't seen in years. He had the uncanny ability to make me feel... like I was the only one who mattered. Well, one of *two* who mattered.

It was hard not to smile back at him. "So, is he mad at me?"

"Who?"

"Who else?" I asked. "Simon."

"Why would he be mad at you?"

"Because I disrespected his authority as the boss."

Adam shook his head. "I think you shocked him more than anything."

I chuckled. "I think I overstepped the friend-guest line."

Adam laughed. "I think you overstepped that line with him more than a week ago."

I laughed, and a familiar voice behind me startled me.

"Something funny?"

I turned to find Simon looking at us, trying not to smile.

Adam answered, "Wil here thinks he might have overstepped some guests-that-are-chefs boundaries." Then Adam chuckled. "He thinks you might be mad at him."

Simon's lips twisted into a pout, though I think he was trying not to smile. "Oh, I am mad at him."

"You are?" I asked, alarmed.

"Oh, sure," Simon said, smiling now. "I think there should be a suitable punishment dealt later tonight."

I chuckled in relief that he was joking and felt heat creep over my cheeks. "Oh."

Adam chuckled, and when Simon asked him if he had any ideas for such a suitable punishment, he nodded. "I think he should sit and watch us." Then he moved in closer, and lowered his voice so only we could hear. "Wil has to watch us fuck. No touching, no jerking off, just watching."

Simon grinned, and I groaned. "That's so not fair."

Simon left us, smiling broadly, to go back to work while Adam taunted me mercilessly with how hot it was going to be, how turned on I was going to be, but really, he had no idea.

Because later that night, when we were in my room, I really wasn't prepared for what it was like. It was hot, and I was so turned on, but it was something more than that.

I sat there in a chair a few feet from the foot of the bed and watched. But they didn't fuck. They made love.

It was slow and tender, and there were so many unspoken words between them. They fucked missionary style with Adam on his back and Simon over him, rocking and thrusting oh-so-slowly. Their hands were on each other's face, thumbing cheekbones, tracing eyebrows, jawlines. They adorned each other with soft kisses, quiet moans, and whispered words.

And I just watched.

It was beautiful.

And it damn near broke my heart.

There was a lump in my throat and my stomach was tied in knots. Tears burned in my eyes and probably would have fallen if Adam hadn't come. With a strangled cry, he lifted his knees higher and his fingers dug into Simon's back as his orgasm rolled through him and smeared between their bodies.

I considered standing up and walking out of the room. It was that one split second when you hesitate and your body doesn't do what your mind is telling it to do. I wanted to leave. I wanted to let them have this moment. I wanted to *not* see what they had when it was something I would never have myself. I wanted to run and hide and scream and cry, and I wanted to punch my ex-lover for never loving me like that.

I wanted... I wanted...

"Stop."

Adam's voice was just a whisper, but Simon stopped immediately and asked him, "Babe, what's wrong?"

Adam turned his face and smiled blissfully at me. "Wil?"

I could barely think straight. "Huh?"

Adam looked up at Simon, who was still leaning over him, still inside him. "I want Wil to join in. It's only right."

Something I couldn't quite recognize flashed across Simon's face, and he slowly pulled out of Adam. He lifted one of Adam's legs and helped him roll over so he could get onto his knees. Adam patted the bed, motioning for me to lie in front of him.

All my willpower to walk out of the door and leave them to it just disappeared. I had my shirt and shorts off and was kneeling on the bed in front of them both before I could blink.

Adam pushed me down onto my back, pulled my aching hard-on out of my briefs, and took me into his mouth. And from the groan that resonated low in his throat and by the way Simon's threw his head back with a look of bliss on his face, I knew Simon was once again buried inside Adam. Adam pulled his mouth off my dick. "Oh, fuck, yes, Sy. Just like that."

Adam hummed and moaned and licked at me once again. "Mmm, Wil, love how you taste." And he took me deep once more. He started to rock with Simon's thrusts, and my cock would fuck his mouth with each pass. Simon lay over Adam's back with his hands hooked under Adam's shoulders, just rocking his hips into him, making Adam moan around me.

With Adam's head low as he sucked me, and with Simon leaning right over him, Simon's eyes locked onto mine.

And he stared at me.

His blue eyes were dark and intense, and he never looked away. He was panting now, and groaning, but he never looked away. His eyes, his stare...

I couldn't look away. Even as the pressure built and the

heat of pleasure crept through my belly and along my spine, I couldn't take my eyes from Simon's. He was looking at me, like... like he looked at Adam.

And with an almost silent scream, Simon's head lolled back and he came. I watched as the planes of his chest expanded, his muscles tight, and Adam groaned as Simon came inside him.

My entire body convulsed, and sensations too pure to contain rolled through me. Adam groaned again when I filled his mouth, my release shooting hot and hard.

When we fell into a heap, we lay there, the three of us, tangled together like we normally did.

But it was different.

It was quiet. No one chuckled, no one joked, and no one said a word.

Something had passed between us, something had shifted. And I wasn't the only one to feel it.

Simon got up from the bed, and instead of going to the bathroom like he normally did, he pulled on his briefs and pants. Adam, who was snuggled into my chest, rolled over to look at him. "What are you doing?"

Simon continued to get dressed. "Gonna head home. Haven't been home for a night in over a week."

"What?" Adam whispered. "Sy, no. Stay here, please."

Simon had his shirt on now. "It's okay. You can stay if you want," he said tightly, and I knew it wasn't okay at all. Then Simon leaned over and kissed Adam's lips. "Love you."

Adam half sat up, and I swear I could hear his heart thumping. It was as though he had to choose between me and his boyfriend. "Sy..."

"It's okay," I finally spoke up, not wanting Adam to think he had to spare my feelings. "Adam, you should go.

You haven't spent a night in your bed for over a week either. You must miss it."

Fuck.

"Anyway," I added, trying to make it easier, "that way I'll get this entire bed to myself. I might even get some sleep."

Adam looked at me and frowned. Then he looked at Simon. And after a long moment, he rolled off the bed and, without a word, got dressed.

Simon waited for him at the door, and Adam picked up his shoes before he walked over to where I was now sitting on the bed. He kissed me, then his eyes dropped, and he whispered, "I'm sorry."

And they left.

Simon hadn't even looked at me.

I crawled into the middle of the bed where Adam normally slept, and just lay there. The bed smelled of them, of us, of what we had just done. And I lay there alone in a bed that was far too big and lonely. I was used to having bodies, touching hands, arms wrapped around me, and the sound of breathing. Now there was silence. And a dull ache in my chest.

Sleep didn't come easily.

CHAPTER EIGHT

I WOKE WITH A START. I had no idea what time it was, but the sun was up and I knew I'd missed my morning run with Simon.

Simon.

Then I remembered. And the heavy lump returned to my chest. I wasn't sure if it had gone anywhere. I'd just had the luxury of being unaware while I slept. With a sigh, I rolled out of bed, showered, and went in search of coffee.

It was later than I'd thought, and I'd missed the breakfast shift altogether. Not that I minded. I'd also missed the likelihood of running into either Simon or Adam, and quite frankly, I wasn't up to seeing either of them.

So I walked straight through, down the stone steps, and onto the beach. And I walked. And I kept walking until I'd stopped thinking and all my head was full of was salt air and Florida sun.

By mid-afternoon when I got back to the hotel, I was starting to feel okay.

Until I saw Adam.

He was behind the bar, cutting up fruit for garnishes.

His eyes lit up when he saw me, then, like he'd remembered the night before, his face dropped. It was unlike him to frown.

I intended to go straight to my room, but his voice stopped me. "Wil?"

I turned to face him. His scruffy blond hair was like it always was, but his eyes were sad, and I couldn't walk away from him. I went back to the bar and sat down. There were other customers around and swimming in the pool, but the bar was empty.

"I'm sorry," he said softly. "I still don't know what happened." He shook his head and his forehead creased. "We were having a great time, and it was hot and intense, then"—he shrugged—"then Simon just... Then it was over."

I nodded, not really knowing what to say.

"I'm sorry," he said again. "I just wish..." He struggled for words again. It was so unlike Adam to be so torn. "I just wish he'd talk to me."

"Simon won't talk to you?"

Adam shook his head. "Not about what happened. I mean, I know something happened during sex. It had to have. Everything was fine before."

I nodded. He was right. I'd seen it. I'd seen it in Simon's eyes. The moment he'd looked at me, with Adam in between us, Simon had stared straight at me. But how did I tell Adam that? How did I explain to him that his boyfriend—the man he obviously loved—had looked at me exactly like he looked at him?

The answer was—I didn't.

The truth was, I was leaving. I meant nothing to them but some temporary fun. I was only a third wheel to play with for the duration of my stay. That was the truth. Not what my heart told me. Not what my heart wanted.

The truth was, I wasn't a part of them.

I looked at Adam, just in time to see his gaze dart over my shoulder. I turned to see Simon standing in the foyer watching us, but he turned on his heel and walked off in the other direction.

I looked back at Adam. He was frowning again. He looked miserable. He took the knife and went back to preparing his garnishes, but it would seem only to do something with his hands.

Needing to know, needing to hear it, I cleared my throat so I could ask, "About tonight...?"

Adam only got through one slice of orange before he put the knife back down and his shoulders fell. His silence and his inability to look at me was answer enough.

I stood up mechanically and nodded. I understood.

Fuck.

Whatever we'd had was done.

It was one thing to assume. It was another to have it confirmed.

Maybe it was the fact I hadn't slept much the night before, or maybe it was the heaviness that settled in my chest and seeped into my bones. Because despite the sounds of Sunday night, of the music and the laughter and living of life outside my door, and despite the bed being too empty, I slept.

I woke up feeling like shit. Figuring a run would do me good, I put on my running gear and headed out. I went left instead of right, away from the headland and the possibility of coming across Simon on his usual run.

Even after only running for a week, I could feel a difference. And I understood why Simon did it. The same reason Adam swam. If not for fitness, to clear the mind.

I got back to the hotel, showered, and dressed. I was starving. I couldn't remember eating the day before, so I dug a book from the bottom of my suitcase, grabbed a plate of fruit, and a cup of coffee, and sat at my usual table overlooking the water.

I'd packed a few books and my iPod thinking I'd be alone for the duration and would need something to do. So to give a clear indication I didn't want to speak to anyone, I deliberately sat with my back to the hotel, put my earphones in, turned the music up, and stuck my nose in the book.

The only person to interrupt me was Sydney. She came to collect my empty plate and cup, but she never spoke. She simply placed a fresh coffee in front of me, patted my arm, and took my dirty dishes away.

If Adam and Simon saw me, watched me, or tried to speak to me, I didn't know.

I did look up occasionally at the people who walked by me, heading toward the beach. The Monday crowd was quieter than the weekend one. A lot of the guests had left, but some new faces arrived.

Sydney interrupted me again, this time with a plate of salad and cold meat and a bottle of water. Though this time she didn't really smile. It was more of a raised eyebrow, and when I pulled one earphone out, her face became stern. "Eat" was all she said, before walking back into the kitchen. She reminded me of Callie. I smiled for the first time in what felt like forever.

It wasn't until I looked at the plate of food that I realized it was lunchtime and I was actually hungry. When I was done with the food and had had enough sun for the day, I stripped off my shirt and dove into the pool to cool off.

Dripping wet, I collected my stuff off the table. I flicked my hands through my hair, trying to dry it as much as possible, and found myself facing the bar. Adam was staring at me. He licked his lips and swallowed hard, and some random guy at the bar smiled at me.

I ignored them both and went to my room.

I wasn't overly hungry and I didn't want to spend the whole evening in my room alone with my thoughts, but I didn't really want company either, so I headed out into the hotel courtyard with my book and iPod. My usual table was taken by people having dinner, so I took an empty one that was unfortunately closer to the bar. Closer to where Adam was. But once again, I sat with my back to the rest of the hotel, put my earphones in, and found my page in the book.

It was maybe an hour later when a tap on the arm startled me. I looked up to see the same guy who'd been sitting at the bar before talking to Adam. He was smiling nervously at me, so I pulled out my earphones and looked at him, waiting for him to speak.

"Uh, hi," he started. Then he motioned toward a chair at my table. "Can I join you?"

I blinked at his request, surprised he'd asked. I would have thought the 'I don't want to talk to anyone' props like earphones and a book spoke for themselves. Apparently not. "Um, sure," I mumbled.

He sat down and started to talk. I tried to listen as he introduced himself. He was twenty-one and here from California on vacation. By himself.

"Are you here with someone?" he asked bluntly.

"Uh..."

"I haven't seen you with anyone all day," he said with no shame in admitting to watching me earlier. "The guy behind the bar said he thought you were here with someone." He looked back toward where Adam stood. I had no doubt he was listening to our conversation.

I looked over at Adam. "Is that what he said?" I asked, unable to keep the disbelief out of my tone. Then, still looking toward Adam, I spoke loud enough for him to hear. "As a matter of fact, I am here alone. Very much so, apparently."

Adam frowned and grimaced, but said nothing.

The guy beside me smiled. "So, did you want to maybe go out? There's a bar called the Green something, I think."

And it suddenly seemed like a great idea. Not so much to go out with what's-his-name but to show Adam and Simon that I could. After wallowing in self-pity for two days, it seemed like a fantastic idea. I nodded at the-guy-whose-name-started-with-K. "Sure. Give me a minute to get changed?" I said, then walked toward my room.

"Sure," he called out after me. "I'll call us a cab."

I threw on my jeans and a white button-down shirt and shoes. I washed my face, brushed my teeth, and hell, I even styled my hair. If I was going to show Adam and Simon that I could have a good time without them, I might as well look good doing it. With a quick glance at my reflection before I walked out of the door, even I thought I didn't look half-bad.

What's-his-name must have thought so too. He was waiting at the bar for me, which was the perfect spot for Adam to see me, and he grinned. "Wow, I thought you looked good half-naked and wet from the pool, but you look pretty good dressed up, too."

I huffed out a laugh at his compliment, but I was glad he'd said it in front of Adam all the same. I could feel Adam's eyes on me, but I looked at the K-named guy. "You ready to go?"

"Wil?"

I turned at the sound of Adam's voice. He still looked tired, but now he looked worried, or bothered, and as though he was trying to think of the right thing to say. Not caring that the K-name guy was right there, he said, "Are you... sure you want to go out?"

"What should I do?" I asked a little too sharply. "Sit here alone all night?"

His face fell and he shook his head. "Wil, don't..."

I couldn't deny seeing him like that and hearing the hurt and concern in his voice tightened my chest. My heart hurt. What I wanted to do was wrap my arms around him and tell him going out with someone else was the *last* thing I wanted to do. But instead I smiled, took what's-his-name's hand, and led him out through the foyer.

When I got to the door, I held it open for my new date to walk through and looked back toward the bar just in time to see Adam throw his dishcloth at the sink with a rather loud "Fuck!"

Then I saw Simon. He was standing near the door to the restaurant, no doubt seeing me leave with another guy and hearing Adam's reaction. I left Adam and Simon staring at each other. The door closed behind me, and I headed toward the waiting cab.

The club itself was just as I remembered it from the week before. It wasn't as busy but still had a half-decent crowd, thumping music, and a swaying dance floor.

I bought us drinks and was lucky enough to hear my date introduce himself to some other guys as Kyle. I'd thought it started with a K. I handed Kyle his drink and sipped on mine as I looked around the club.

Kyle stepped in close so I could hear him over the music. "You've been here before?"

I nodded. "Last week."

Kyle nodded and moved even closer, this time putting his free hand on my hip. "Thanks for the drink."

I guessed it was supposed to be seductive, the way his lips brushed my ear, and the way his hand held my hips in place. I could certainly feel him against me. I could even smell his cologne.

But it did nothing for me.

It was just... wrong.

I smiled politely at him and put a little distance between us. "No problem," I said quickly. "Want another one?"

I didn't really give him time to answer. I just went back to the bar. I figured I'd need a few drinks to loosen up and possibly even warm up to Kyle.

After the next drink, he wanted to dance, and I obliged. It was okay. Our bodies touched and his hands were on me as we moved to the music, but it wasn't the same. He pulled us off the dance floor and leaned in to speak in my ear. "You don't really want to be here tonight, do you?"

I sighed and shook my head. "Not really, no."

He smiled kindly at me. "You don't have to stay."

So I didn't stay. I wrote down the hotel address, just in case he didn't know it, and gave him a twenty for the cab fare. Considering he'd asked me out and I was bailing, it was the least I could do. And I left.

The hotel was dark by the time I got back, and thankfully I didn't see Adam or Simon. I crawled into the cold bed and stared at the wall till morning.

Just before sunrise, I was dressed and out running. The sky was a pretty palate of pinks, purples, and oranges before it smeared into an early morning blue. I was tired and probably not fit for running, but I pushed through it and ran anyway.

I forced myself to eat some fruit for breakfast. Well, Sydney forced me. But it came with coffee, so I didn't object too much. I skipped lunch, and too tired to walk the beach, I only came out of my room after the lunch crowd had gone. Armed with my book and iPod, I found my table and sat in the sun, settling in for what I hoped would be a few hours of uninterrupted peace.

But without a word and without an invitation, Adam sat down in the chair next to me. When I looked at him, my stomach dropped. He looked... sick.

I frowned at him. "Adam, when was the last time you ate? Or slept?"

He ignored my question. "Sy won't tell me what's wrong," he whispered. "He's really stressed out. There's a meeting with the owners here tomorrow and he's got that to deal with... but he's miserable. He keeps saying it's nothing. He tries to smile. He tries to act like he's okay..."

"And what about you?"

Adam shrugged. "I thought what we had was it, ya know?"

My heart ached for him. "I'm sure once this meeting with the owners is done, he'll be back to normal," I told him, trying to comfort him.

Adam stared at me for a long moment, then he shook his head. His voice was just a whisper. "I wasn't talking about just me and him."

Oh.

He meant the three of us. He thought the three of us had something special.

I smiled sadly. "I did too," I admitted quietly. "I know it was just a week, but it was... intense."

Adam looked at me and nodded quickly. "I know. That's what I thought. I *thought* that's what Simon thought."

"I'm sorry, Adam. I really am. If I had known it was going to cause problems between you, I wouldn't have agreed..."

"No, Wil," he said, shaking his head. His eyes were a wide and honest blue. "I don't regret it. In fact, I... I wouldn't change it."

I huffed out a sigh, resigned. "Neither would I."

Adam's face twisted. It wasn't right to see him hurting like this. I wanted to make it better for him. "Adam, you and Simon were the best things to ever happen to me. I don't regret it, not a second of it. But it would have been nice to leave here on a high."

"I know," he whispered.

Then a silence fell between us. I guessed at this point there wasn't much left to say. It wasn't me or Adam who needed to do the talking.

"Do you want me to try and talk to Simon?"

Adam shook his head, and his voice was barely a whisper as he said, "He's got a lot on his mind right now, with the owners and everything..."

And that answer just pissed me off. Simon was the one who had put us in this mess and he got out of it scot-free.

Adam looked out toward the water and changed the subject. "That Kyle kid told me you left him at the club. Said your heart wasn't in it."

I pushed down the twisted lump of sudden anger in my gut, but my tone still had bite. "No, you wanna know why? Because he smelled wrong. He felt wrong. Because there wasn't two of him. Even if there had been, it wouldn't have been the right two." I stood up and bit down my anger. It wasn't Adam I was angry at. I sighed, tired and frustrated. I leaned over and touched his arm. "Fuck, Adam, I'm sorry. You don't need this from me."

He looked at me with his sad blue eyes, and it squeezed my heart.

"You have no idea just how sorry I am," I said.

I stood up and walked away, but I'd swear I heard him say, "But I do."

CHAPTER NINE

AFTER MY RUN, I showered and didn't bother with breakfast. It was Wednesday, so I knew Adam wasn't working, and I didn't really feel up to seeing him. On my second-to-last full day there, I wanted to get out and do something.

So I took in some more sights, mostly walking the sidewalks, window-shopping, taking in the sounds and smells of downtown Key West. I bought a few souvenirs and a few trinkets for Callie, but by lunchtime, I found myself at Dee's café.

She grinned when I walked in, but when she realized Simon and Adam weren't with me, her smile slowly died.

She served me coffee I didn't ask for but gladly accepted. "Tell me what happened," she said sternly.

I tried to smile for her but couldn't get it right, so I gave up. I shrugged instead. "I'm not sure, to be honest."

She frowned before she pouted her thick lips. "And you haven't been eating," she stated simply. Then she mumbled something about silly boys with a shake of her head as she scribbled something down on her order pad, ripped off a page, and handed it to the cook through the service window.

When she looked at me, she sighed. "So you don't know what happened? Or you just don't want to tell me?"

I did smile this time. Dee was abrupt and bossy, blunt and loud. I liked her.

"Things were going great," I finally admitted. "Too great, probably. It was kinda perfect. But then three days ago, something changed for Simon, and he..." I wasn't sure exactly how much I should be telling her, so I trailed off and sipped my coffee instead. "Well, it's not perfect anymore."

Dee nodded. "Perfect, you say? Let me tell you something about Simon," she said. "I've known him most of his life, and he's a good man. It wasn't easy for him when he first realized he was gay, and he tried the straight thing for a little while, and well, that was... disastrous." She smiled to herself.

Then she was serious again. "But he's lucky. He comes from a good family who love him, unlike Adam's family." She shook her head. "And yes, he could have easily gone to work with his father and cruised through life, but he's stood on his own two feet. That takes guts. He's a good businessman. He's smart and he's funny as hell when he lets his guard down."

I looked at her, wondering how telling me all his good traits—some I'd known, some I hadn't—was supposed to help.

"But, Wil," she said seriously. "Simon is a *lot* of things. But he's not perfect. I saw how you were looking at him last week, all dreamy-eyed like the man could do no wrong. Well, sugar, he's just a man. And Lord knows how the three of you can keep each other in line. I have enough trouble with one!"

I snorted, and Dee laughed. She walked away but came back with a plate of food and put it in front of me.

I raised both eyebrows and looked up at her. We both knew I'd never ordered the meal. She smiled. "It's a house specialty."

"It's the biggest burger I've ever seen!"

Dee laughed. "It will do you good. Don't argue with me."

I chuckled despite myself. "Um, thanks?"

Dee said, "I'll ask you one thing, Wil. Don't answer me until after you've eaten, but tell me this... Now what Simon and Adam have is the real deal. You and I both know that. And that's what you want. Honey, we all do. But my question is this. Do you want what they have with someone else? Can you picture yourself with another man? With another two men?"

She turned to some other customers and left me alone with the world's biggest burger and an awful lot to think about.

And Dee was right. The burger was good. Not that I could finish it. Not even close. But it was the right mix of textures, spicy, and savory.

"Enjoy it?" Dee asked when I finally pushed the plate away.

I groaned and rubbed my stomach. Maybe after not eating a great deal in three days, having such a huge meal hadn't been a very good idea. "Oh my God," I groaned again. "So good."

Dee laughed. "Soul food, my friend. Have you thought about what I said?"

I took a sip of water and nodded. "I have. But first, Dee, tell me about Adam."

Dee called out to the other staff there that she was taking a break, and she sat across the booth from me. She smiled. "It's not really my story to tell, sugar."

I nodded. "Well, it's just every time the word *family* is mentioned, he clams up. You mentioned before his family wasn't like Simon's, so it doesn't take rocket science to work it out."

Dee frowned and was quiet for a moment while she chose her words carefully. She shook her head. "It's something I'll never understand." Her island accent was thicker when she spoke passionately. "How a mother can carry a child, give him life, and love him, only to disown him at seventeen because of who he fell in love with. A parent's love is supposed to be *un*conditional. It's not selective."

Dee took a breath to calm down. This was obviously a subject she didn't take lightly. "Adam came from New York originally. He was an A student and champion swimmer, apparently."

Ah well, that explained his love for swimming.

"His parents were conservatives and when they caught him kissing a boy, well... well, it didn't go down very well. And he found himself here."

She'd told me enough. I didn't need to hear any more. Adam had been disowned at seventeen. *Fuck.*

It made my heart hurt for Adam just that little bit more.

It explained a lot, though. The way Adam seemed like he could handle any crowd, like he'd seen it all before and how a simple smile could get him what he wanted. He was street-smart. But it also explained why Simon was protective of him and grounded him.

It explained a lot.

"What about your family, Wil?" Dee asked. "What's your story?"

"My parents died just over two years ago. I was an only child."

"Oh, sugar, I'm sorry," Dee said, genuinely concerned.

"It's okay." I smiled at her. "It was a car accident. One day they're there, and the next they're not."

Dee frowned, but I just shrugged. "I set up my own restaurant not long after that. It was kind of the push I needed to do something for myself..."

"Got a boyfriend back home?"

I snorted. "In *my* hometown? Not likely. Had a secret lover, I guess you'd call it. Not a boyfriend the likes of Simon and Adam, more of a sex-when-he-wanted-it kind of thing." I shook my head at how ludicrous it sounded, even to me. "Very, very much in the closet. But he dumped me when I was outed."

Dee's eyes widened. "Really?"

I snorted again. "That's only the half of it." I gave her a brief rundown of how the entire town, all but my best friend Callie, refused to eat at my restaurant because I was gay— well, at least while I was there. Callie seemed to be doing okay with it on her own.

I think I shocked poor Dee into silence.

After she blinked and opened and closed her mouth a few times, she finally exhaled slowly. "Just what exactly are you going home to?"

I thought about it for a moment, and unable to give a straight answer, I shrugged. "I don't know."

She shook her head and sighed. "Oh, Wil. You certainly went from the pan into the fire down here, didn't you?"

I huffed. "I guess I did."

Dee smiled and shook her head at me. "I better get back to work."

"Don't you want to know my answer?"

"Answer to what, sugar?"

"Your question. Earlier. You asked if I wanted what Simon and Adam have."

Dee smiled knowingly. "That wasn't what I really asked. What I asked was do you want what they have, not with someone else, but *with them?* Do you want to be *with* them?"

"Oh."

"And, sugar, the answer to that is written all over your face."

———

I got back to the hotel late in the afternoon, not long before the dinner shift was supposed to start. I intended to head straight for my room, but walking through the foyer, I heard Simon's voice.

The other guests seemed oblivious. Maybe it was just Simon's voice and I couldn't *not* hear him. He sounded less than pleased. Actually, he sounded livid.

I walked a bit farther around and I could see him then. He was pacing in the kitchen with his cell phone to his ear. And he was furious. He was keeping his voice down, but there was no mistaking the tone.

"Who the hell am I going to get on this short notice, Miguel? I've got the owners of the hotel due here in half a fucking hour for a meeting to decide if they're selling to Hartley! You knew this dinner meeting was on! You know how important this is!"

I walked up beside Adam, who was watching. "What's up?"

Adam looked over at me and smiled. Almost. He kept his voice low while Simon was on the phone. "Miguel, the asshole, phoned in just now saying he couldn't make it in tonight. He was supposed to be here already. He's doing it to get back at Sy. He knows how important tonight is, and after Simon reprimanded him about his attitude this week, he's a no-show. What he's really doing is just proving what an asshole he is. We even called in poor Syd, but it's just with this meeting..."

I turned and left them in the kitchen, dumped my shopping bags on the bed in my room, changed out of my cargos and into jeans and my lace-up leather shoes. It wasn't exactly work attire, but it was better than nothing.

I went back into the kitchen. Simon was off the phone, now mumbling to himself in the cool storage room.

Ignoring him, I walked into the kitchen prep area. A rather flustered Sydney looked at me. "Syd, where can I get a chef's shirt?"

She smiled. "Uniforms are in the back storeroom."

I grabbed one, then returned to the kitchen, buttoning up the second row of buttons. Simon was now in the prep area, rifling through one of the drawers and looking for God only knew what. He looked up and stared at me. "What are you doing?"

I ignored him and asked Sydney, "Where's the menu? Recipe cards?"

She pointed to a folder on the far wall filled with standard recipe cards. All restaurants that had changing staff used systems like this, so when the staff changed with each shift, the recipes didn't. "It's the one on top," Syd called out, and I pulled it out and started to read. I could feel Simon's eyes boring into the side of my head.

His voice was eerily calm. "Wil, I said, what are you doing?"

I looked at him then. That was the first thing he'd said to me in three days. "Oh, you're talking to me now?"

He gritted his teeth and walked right up to me. "Wil..."

God, he had *no* right to be angry at me. I'd done nothing wrong. And he wanted to know what I was doing? So I told him. "I'm trying to read the fucking recipe so I know what to cook for your meeting, that's what I'm doing!"

We stood, barely inches apart, chests heaving. He was suited up for this meeting. His black hair was styled and spiked. His nostrils flared, and his eyes were a steely blue.

He was beautiful.

But I was so fucking angry with him. The last three days' worth of angry, but this was neither the place nor the time.

"Now, if you don't mind, I have work to do, so get out of the kitchen."

He stared at me for a long moment before turning on his heel and walking out. He was pissed off. Fucking angry would be a more apt description. And so was I.

I looked up to see Adam standing in the doorway to the kitchen as Simon stalked past him. Adam was a little shocked, but when his eyes landed on me, he smiled.

"Jesus," Sydney whispered beside me.

"I'm sorry." I put the recipes down and looked at her. "That wasn't very professional. I'm not normally so... angry."

Sydney snorted as she stirred the pot of sauce on the stove. "Neither is he," she said with a pointed nod in the direction Simon went. "But something's been bothering him for the last three days. He's been a cranky shit."

I huffed sarcastically. "Tell me about it."

Sydney looked up at me from the stove. "I don't suppose him being cranky has anything to do with you and Adam both being so out of sorts?"

I looked at her, and for a long moment, I wondered how

I should answer. She just rolled her eyes and went back to stirring the sauce. "What the hell is it with men? You get stressed and get skinny. Women get stressed, eat ice cream, and put on ten pounds."

I laughed despite my mood. "Yes, I suppose I should thank you for bringing me lunch and coffee yesterday and ordering me to eat."

She snorted. "Yeah, like I *suppose* I should thank you for helping me tonight."

I chuckled, sincerely this time. "Well, if you did thank me, I'd say you were most welcome."

Sydney looked at me and grinned. "Likewise, Wil. Likewise."

I walked into the cool storage to get the salmon, and when I came back out, Adam was walking in. He looked so tired, and now agitated.

"They're here," he said, looking back out to the tabled area. "There're four of them—the two owners, an accountant, and a lawyer. Simon's with them." Adam shook his head. "I hope he'll be okay."

I put the salmon steaks down on the counter. "Adam, he'll be just fine."

"I couldn't do that," he said with a shake of his head. "Sit out there with the bigwigs talking business like he does."

I said, "Adam, if you sat out there in that meeting, you'd win them over with your smile alone."

His grin was slow to spread, then quick to go. "Maybe I should sit at the bar and give the lawyer fuck-me eyes from across the room. He seemed the type."

Sydney and I both laughed, and Adam chuckled. Then he sighed. "Can I hang out in here with you guys?" he asked. "I'm not working. It's too quiet upstairs and Simon's down here, well, out there," he said, looking out to the tables. Then he looked at me, "And you're in here..."

Sydney spoke first, "Can you wash dishes?"

Adam mock pouted. "I'm a man of many talents."

He was soon up to his elbows in suds but seemed the happiest he'd been in two days. Syd and I worked well together. We just gelled.

And for the next two hours, I made the best three-course meal of my life for the four VIPs—five including Simon. I helped Syd push out appetizers, entrées, and desserts when I could, and we still managed to have a good time doing it.

And by the time it was all over and we'd cleaned up, the hotel was quiet. There were still a few guys out near the pool; some were even dancing. Adam collected three beers from the bar, and not wanting the owners to see staff sitting around after their shifts had finished, we pulled up stools and sat in the kitchen.

We talked and joked around. It felt so good to laugh. It seemed Adam had even forgotten his troubles and told Syd and me funny stories till our sides hurt.

Then Simon came into the kitchen with a tray of the empty dessert plates in his hands, and our laughter died. He stopped awkwardly and looked at us three, but his eyes lingered on me and Adam. Before any one of us could speak, he put the tray down on the counter. "I don't know what you put in that dessert crème, Wil, but it was... um, it was something special. They're still out there talking about it." He offered me a small smile and announced to no one in particular, "We're just wrapping up now."

We all watched him walk back out to where the meeting was almost done. Adam said, "I think he just complimented your cooking."

Syd laughed. "What was that white crème, anyway?"

I smiled at her. "Wanna try it? There's some left over." I didn't wait for an answer. I just went into the fridge and came out with the remaining desserts while Adam grabbed three plates and three spoons.

"I make this for Callie back home," I told them. "If I ever need to apologize for something, it's usually with a batch of this." I put some fresh raspberries on a plate, scooped a dollop of the white chocolate and vanilla bean crème on top, and handed it to Syd. "Try that."

Adam and I both watched her, and the second the flavors hit her tongue, she moaned.

I laughed and told Adam, "That's exactly what Callie says."

Adam laughed, and I served up the same for him, then me. Adam hummed and nodded. "This is good," he said with a mouthful.

Watching him eat the dessert was both wonderful—and complete and utter torture. The way he hummed, watching the spoon go into his mouth, how he licked his lips, how there were traces of white crème on his tongue made my cock stir.

I think I groaned.

I was so transfixed on Adam, I didn't realize Simon had walked in and was watching us. Adam just looked at him and smiled. "See what you mean, Sy. This is delicious."

Sydney stood up and shook her head, telling Simon, "It sure was. But watching Wil watching Adam eat it is worse than watching porn."

I choked on a raspberry, and Syd just laughed. She put her plate in the sink, threw her empty beer bottle in the trash can, then clapped her hand on my shoulder. "Wil, my friend, you can cook with me anytime." Then as she walked out, she added, "As long as you make that dessert." And she was gone.

I stood up and put my plate in the sink, and the fun of the evening was over. As the three of us stood in the kitchen, none of us really knew what to say, or how to start. My heart was in my throat.

Adam spoke first. His voice was low. "So the meeting went okay?"

Simon nodded and shrugged one shoulder. "Um, can we talk about that later?" His entire demeanor had changed. He wasn't angry or distant anymore. He was quiet. Maybe even sorry.

"Oh, okay," Adam offered. "Sure."

Simon looked at me. "I owe you big time."

I picked up Adam's plate and put it in the sink and looked at Simon. The fight had left me too, so my voice was low. "You don't owe me anything." Then I pointed a glance at Adam. "You owe Adam. Not me. You owe him an explanation and an apology."

Adam looked at me, wide-eyed and shocked. Simon looked at the floor and nodded. "You're right. I do." He swallowed then looked at Adam. "Can we talk? Please?"

"Of course we can," Adam said, moving to slide his hand along Simon's jaw. "Of course we can."

I smiled at them, though they didn't see, and I walked toward the door. Simon's voice stopped me. "You too, Wil. You need to hear this."

I blinked in shock. "Oh, are you sure?"

Simon smiled sadly. "Only if you want to."

"Okay," I said, still unsure of what he had to say that could possibly change anything.

CHAPTER TEN

I UNLOCKED the door to my room and walked in. Adam followed me, and Simon came in last. He seemed very nervous, and both Adam and I watched him. And waited. He bit his lip and his brow creased. It was then I realized how tired he looked too. He had darkened circles under his eyes, but it was more than that. He looked worried.

He licked his lips, and spoke to Adam. "I'm sorry," he started, and the floodgates opened. "I'm so sorry. I freaked out and I got scared. I didn't think it was a good idea to continue with Wil because I was worried I'd lose you, and I ended up pushing you away. I really fucked things up, and I'm sorry I hurt you. I love you, Adam, I really do, and I don't want to lose you."

Adam cupped Simon's face. "Why would you lose me? Sy, you need to talk to me, not push me away."

Simon nodded, his head still in Adam's hands. "I know. I'm sorry."

Adam frowned. "Why didn't you think it was a good idea to keep seeing Wil?"

Simon swallowed loudly. His eyes darted to mine, then

back to Adam. "Because... because... it was supposed to be fun. It was supposed to be a threesome fling for a night or two, then it was for a week. And then we spent all that time together, and the three of us really clicked."

Adam shook his head, confused. "What went wrong?"

Simon's face twisted and he frowned. But he looked at me, then at Adam, then to the floor in front of him and shrugged. "I started to fall in love with him."

My lungs didn't work. My brain couldn't function. But my heart beat double time, thumping hard against my ribs.

Simon quickly looked back to Adam. "I'm sorry. I never meant for it to happen. It doesn't mean I love you any less, Ad. I can't explain it... It's like... I don't know... It's like..."

Adam finished for him. "It's like you love two people exactly the same."

Simon nodded. "I'm sorry, baby. I just thought if I put some distance between us, if I waited until Wil went home, I'd be okay and you'd never know." Simon looked at me then. "But it was horrible, and I was an asshole, and I'm sorry. I didn't know what to do... I didn't know how to deal with it."

Adam smiled. "You silly man, you should have told me. You should have told Wil."

I still don't think I'd blinked.

Simon seemed hopeful as he looked at a happy Adam. "You're not mad?"

Adam laughed. "Why would I be mad? Sy, of course you have feelings for Wil." Adam looked at me and grinned. "He's gorgeous, smart, funny, and great in bed..."

I finally got my mouth to work. "Huh?"

Adam chuckled at me. "And apparently at a loss for words."

I stammered, "I, um, I'm not, um... I'm not sure I

follow..." I shook my head and started again. "I'm not sure I understand."

Adam walked over to me, bringing Simon with him. Adam traced his fingers along my jaw. "I'm pretty sure Sy wants you to kiss him."

Simon's eyes widened. I'm sure they matched mine. And without a conscious decision to do so, I touched the side of his face. Simon leaned into my palm and sighed.

So I kissed him.

I touched my lips to his softly at first, pulling his bottom lip between mine, then kissing him a little deeper. And when my tongue touched his, he moaned and opened his mouth, letting me devour him.

So I did.

My body reacted to his taste, his touch, and the feel of him against me. It felt so right.

Then the kiss changed. Simon's hands held my face, then my hair. I could feel his fingers tighten as he kissed me harder. I could feel his urgency. I could feel the emotion. He'd never kissed me like that before.

Adam whimpered beside us. "You're so hot together."

I couldn't help but smile against Simon's mouth, and I pulled away to breathe. But Adam wrapped his hand around my neck and pulled me in for a kiss. Slow and languid, his tongue pressed against mine, as though he was savoring the very taste of me.

It was a different kiss. He tasted different than Simon, he kissed differently. But no less perfectly. It felt right. It felt right with Simon, and it felt just as right with Adam.

I had one arm around Simon and the other around Adam, and they each had an arm around me. The three of us stood against one another, kissing and holding for all we were worth. We'd swap mouths, kiss down necks, hold a little tighter, and kiss a little harder.

Kissing them together, being with them together, was right.

It felt natural and real. And perfect.

Then it slowed down. The need and the urgency became tender and gentle, warm and lovely until our foreheads rested together and we caught our breaths.

Simon's eyes were closed, and he swayed, falling into us. Adam and I both steadied him, and his eyes opened wearily. "I'm so tired. There's so much I want to say," he murmured. Then he smirked. "So much I want to do with both of you. But I'm so tired."

Adam smiled. "Come on, baby," he said, pulling Simon over to the bed to undress him. "You're exhausted. Did you sleep at all last night?"

Simon shook his head. "Mm-mm, no." He shucked out of his shirt, and his pants fell to his feet. He sat down on the edge of the bed in his briefs and he looked up at Adam. "I just watched you sleep. Wondered what you'd say, what you'd tell me, if you'd leave me..."

"Oh, Sy," Adam whispered and knelt at his feet. "Never, baby."

Adam undid Simon's shoes, peeling them off one at a time. Simon looked up at me, and his words were slurred. "Can we talk tomorrow?"

I really wanted to talk tonight. I still hadn't answered him. Not that I had any clue what to say. But I hadn't said anything. I looked at Simon as he sat there with Adam taking care of him. He was utterly and devastatingly beautiful. And almost asleep. "We'll talk in the morning," I offered.

Simon nodded. "Sorry, haven't slept. So tired." His

blinks were getting longer, his head seemed too heavy ,and when Adam pulled back the covers, Simon simply curled up on the bed.

Adam smiled and hurried to get undressed, then scrambled onto the bed. In the middle. In his spot. He was grinning now and patted the bed beside him. "Come on, Wil."

I smiled at him, stripped down to my briefs, and climbed onto the bed. Adam snuggled down with his back against Simon, who, even with his eyes closed, nuzzled his nose behind Adam's ear. Simon's arm quickly wrapped around Adam, but then his hand waved in the air, blindly looking for something.

So I gave him my hand.

And on the verge of sleep, with his eyes closed, Simon threaded his fingers with mine. He was utterly exhausted. With the last two days, not sleeping at all the night before, the stress of the dinner meeting with his bosses, and the added worry of how Adam would react to learning he had feelings for me, it wasn't surprising he was worn out. The stress and the guilt must have weighed a ton.

It was all so surreal. Simon... had feelings for me.

Adam sighed, making me look from Simon to him. His eyes were closed, but he was smiling. He was so cute with his blond, scruffy hair and beautiful lips. He still looked tired, but lying between Simon and me, he looked happy. Then his eyes half opened, and he murmured, "He's falling in love with you."

I nodded, not really sure what to say.

I still hadn't said anything about it. Not to Simon when he'd said it; not to Adam. I'd never really had anyone declare feelings for me. Lord knows Rod never had, and there hadn't really ever been anyone else...

Adam smiled and closed his eyes, but his arm slid

around my waist, and he pulled me against him. He nestled himself into my neck, with mine and Simon's joined hands at his chest. He sighed contentedly against my skin. Then he whispered sleepily, "And, Wil?"

"Yeah?"

"He's not the only one."

I sucked back a breath at Adam's words, but his arm tightened around me and he wriggled himself closer to me. His breathing soon evened out, and I knew he'd fallen asleep. I was too tired to try to make sense of it. It had been an emotionally draining two days, and I turned Simon's and now Adam's words over in my head.

I started falling in love with him...

He's not the only one...

I didn't want to think about the possibility that they could be falling in love with me or that I could be falling for them. Not one of them. Not just Adam, not just Simon. But both of them. *Them.* I didn't want to think about how my heart thumped differently when I saw them, how my skin tingled when they were near, or how the very thought of them made me smile. How I'd never experienced anything like it before. So fast, so intense. So very real.

And the likelihood I would never find it again.

I didn't want to think about what it meant. Because I was no longer counting down days until I went back to Alabama. I was counting down hours.

I closed my eyes, and instead of thinking about what anything meant, I savored the warmth of their bodies and listened to the sound of them breathing.

I slept like a baby.

Simon didn't go running, and Adam didn't swim. It was as though we knew our time was running out, and as the sun came up, the three of us stayed in bed.

We still hadn't talked about what had been said. Adam had woken up firmly pressed between us, and he soon had us too worked up to think about anything else. He was impossible to deny. But he didn't want to stay in the middle of us. Oh no, that was where he wanted *me*, he said.

In between them.

So that was where they put me.

Condoms and lube applied, Adam was on his back, with his knees up near his chest, and my hands were at the sides of his head, holding his legs back with my shoulders. I was buried inside him as far as I could go, while Simon took me from behind.

We'd done that position before. Actually, the very first time we'd been together had been like that, me fucking Adam while Simon fucked me.

But this was very different.

It was... intimate, and slow. It wasn't fucking at all.

Adam touched my face with one hand and held Simon's hand with his other. Simon was leaning over me with his free arm wrapped around my waist, pushing so far inside me and rolling his hips like he was trying to crawl inside me, pushing me into Adam.

It was gentle and tender, grinding and pushing, and filling the room with low moans and whimpers. I kissed Adam, his mouth and his jaw, while Simon kissed my shoulder and nipped at the back of my neck.

They locked gazes over my shoulder, and I could see it in Adam's eyes. So close, right in front of me, so full of emotion and wonder.

Then he looked at me the same. He thrust his thumb into my mouth, so without taking my eyes from his, I sucked and twirled my tongue around his thumb. And with every measured thrust, Simon kissed my neck.

"Oh, fuck," Adam moaned. "Both of you. Oh my God."

"Yeah," Simon groaned, hot and rough in my ear. "So good. Both of you." He thrust a little sharper, making me buck into Adam.

And it set him off. "Oh, yes! Right there!"

So Simon did it again. Again and again, until Adam arched underneath me. His ass clenched around me, his cock spilled between us, and Simon kept thrusting into me, making me fuck Adam harder through his orgasm, drawing it out of him, making Adam groan.

He was spent, boneless, panting, chuckling, and moaning. Finally his legs splayed apart, sliding down my sides to the bed, and my cock slipped out of him. Simon pulled out of me and tapped the palm of his hand against my ass. "Roll over for me."

Falling to the side of a blissed-out Adam, I did as Simon wanted. I lay on my back, and he positioned himself between my thighs. He lifted my legs, pushing them back toward my chest, and he slid back inside me, filling me so completely.

He leaned over me, fused his mouth to mine, and kissed me so profoundly. He held my face like I meant the world to him, and he pushed every inch of his cock deeper and deeper inside me.

And he was everywhere, and everything. All I could feel, all I could taste.

"You're so hot together," Adam murmured beside us, threading his fingers through our hair.

Simon turned his head to kiss Adam, and I pushed my

head back against the pillows with a low moan. Then Adam was kissing me, thrusting his tongue into my mouth while Simon thrust his cock in my ass.

I was so full of both of them. They were over me and inside me. It was overwhelming, and crushing, and perfect.

So perfect.

Simon leaned back on his haunches, still thrusting inside me, and he slid off my condom and fisted my cock.

"Oh fuck," I gasped.

Simon's head fell back. He was panting, and his thrusts were harder, more erratic. "Wil, baby, I need you to come for me."

Adam knelt beside Simon then and patted his hand off my cock. Leaning down over my leg, he took my aching dick into his mouth.

I almost bucked us off the bed, moaning and grunting without shame. Simon fucked me harder, deeper while Adam sucked me all the way down. And my body took over.

I couldn't have stopped if I'd wanted to.

I came so hard. So fucking hard. Painless fire ripped through me, and I shot hot and thick down Adam's throat with a roar. Simon gripped my hips and pinned me to him, holding onto me while wave after wave of pleasure crashed through me. And only when I was done did he fuck me until he came.

I'd never experienced anything like it.

The three of us lay on the bed naked, sated and sweaty. It was a peaceful silence. Simon was tracing patterns on Adam's chest, while Adam was staring at the ceiling, a million miles away.

Then Simon moaned. "Ugh. I wish I could spend all day here with you both."

I propped my head up on my hand so I could see Simon

over Adam, who was—as always—lying between us. "So did the owners tell you exactly what they wanted all these reports for?"

"No, just gave me a list of financials to have ready. They didn't say exactly. But I better get started," he said, rolling off the bed.

"Don't go."

Simon stopped just short of the bathroom and looked at Adam. He'd been quiet so long, his words surprised us both. Simon smiled at him. "I have to go, babe. I've got all those financial reports to organize. I know we need to talk, and we will. You guys could come with me into the office to keep me company…" Simon's words died away when he realized Adam wasn't talking to him.

Adam was looking at me.

"Oh," Simon said like he understood. Then he looked at me. "Oh."

I shot Adam a look. "Me?"

Adam rolled his eyes. "There's not a fourth person in here, is there?"

Simon's trip to the bathroom was seemingly forgotten. He walked back to the bed and waited for Adam to explain.

Adam looked at me and said it again, "Don't go."

I shook my head. "Adam—"

"I'm asking you not to leave," he cut me off. "I'm asking you to stay, Wil. Don't go back to Alabama."

"Adam," I said. "It's not that simple."

"Yes, it is," he replied. "It's exactly that simple."

I looked at Simon, and his eyes were darting between me and Adam. "Sy?"

He swallowed hard and I could see his chest rise and fall with each breath. I could almost hear his mind racing.

He stared at Adam for a long second, then he looked at me. "Stay."

Oh, hell.

Adam grinned. "We just found you. I know it's a lot to ask, but I don't want to lose you. *We* don't want to lose you." Then Adam sat up on his knees and looked to Simon. "I'm right, aren't I? This is right, isn't it? We're supposed to be together."

Simon looked at Adam and nodded. Then he looked at me. "Do you want to? Stay, that is? With us? To be a part of us?"

Adam added, "Live with us, work with us. Here, at the hotel."

I looked at them both and thought about what they were proposing. The three of us, together, as a permanent thing. "Sounds perfect."

Adam buzzed with excitement and started to bounce on his knees, but then he stopped and frowned. "There's a *but* coming, isn't there?"

I gave him a sad smile. "But I have a business, a house."

"And nothing else!" Adam threw back at me. "You said yourself your business was as good as over, Wil. You can work here, with us! You need a chef, don't you Sy?"

We turned to Simon. He nodded. "I do, but I don't expect you... I don't want you to think that's what this is about. But the job's yours if you want it."

Jesus. They're serious.

Adam shook his head. "It scares me to think you'll be going back to a town that wants you gone, Wil. What if someone tries to hurt you?"

"Adam," Simon stopped him.

"What?" Adam cried. "You can't tell me you're not worried about some homophobic rednecks waiting for him to get home. Doesn't it bother you that he's prepared to go back to a closeted half-life?"

"Adam," I said. "I'm sure it'll be okay."

"You can't be sure!" he answered, shaking his head. "So then don't stay with us and don't be a part of us, if that's what you're worried about. Get a job somewhere else, but just don't go back there." His eyes were wide. "Please."

I wanted to tell him, reassure him that it would be okay and I'd be perfectly safe. But the truth was I didn't know for sure.

Simon's voice startled me. "What time does your flight leave tomorrow?"

"Six a.m."

"How much time will you need? To think about it?"

"Um..."

Simon put his hand out to Adam and said, "Come on, Ad. Wil needs some time on his own. He can't make this decision with us around."

I could see Adam was torn. He didn't want to leave, but he knew Simon had a point. So they got dressed while I sat in shock on the bed.

Adam looked at me. "I know it's a lot to ask, and I know we haven't talked about anything from last night," he said with a frown. "And we really need to talk about how you feel about us." He shrugged. "But I know you feel the same, Wil. I can see it in your eyes."

Simon smiled.

I opened my mouth to say something, anything, but Adam kept talking. "But you need some time, and I understand... It's an awful lot to take in. But, Wil, you know how we feel about you."

Simon walked over to where I sat on the bed with nothing but a sheet puddled over my hips. He knelt on the bed, leaned over, and pressed his lips to mine. "If you need to talk about anything or ask any questions, we'll be through the foyer and up the stairs. There's two doors—one says office, one says residence. Knock on both if you have to. I know it's quick and you've had two point five seconds to think about it, but we're very serious about this. We can do this, the three of us," he said with a nod. "Take your time. We want you to make the right decision."

I nodded, though my head was spinning.

I looked at Adam, and he smiled. "You know, if you want me to stay and help you... make up your mind..." He trailed off suggestively.

Simon tried not to smile as he pulled Adam out of the door. Then I was alone with an awful lot to think about.

Two minutes later there was a knock at the door, and I still hadn't moved. My brain was stuck in neutral. I edged off the bed, wrapped a towel around my waist, and opened the door.

It was Adam, handing over a cup of steaming coffee. "Made a decision yet?"

Simon came from nowhere. "You said you wouldn't ask. You said you'd just drop off the coffee and leave him alone." Simon apologized to me, rolling his eyes, and pulled Adam by the hand, leading him away.

I stood in the doorway, watching them. Adam looked over his shoulder at me and waved. It made me laugh. I shut the door and sipped the coffee. He'd made it just how I liked it. They wanted me to stay. To really stay. To live with them, to work with them. To be a part of them. To be a permanent threesome. Boyfriends. Partners.

Holy fuck.

But I wasn't stupid. I knew it wouldn't be easy. I knew it

would take a lot of hard work. And my restaurant... my house...

And the one person in that town who'd miss me. The one person I told everything to, who understood me, who knew me. The one person who wouldn't hesitate to tell me I was being a fucking idiot.

I pulled out my phone, and dialed.

"Hello?"

"Hi, Callie. It's me."

CHAPTER ELEVEN

THERE WAS A LONG SILENCE. "WHAT?"

I sighed and repeated what I'd already said. "If I was considering selling the restaurant, would you be in a position to buy it?"

There was another beat of silence. "Wil, what are you doing?"

"I'm not sure yet," I answered honestly. I wasn't sure. I didn't have a clue. "I'm just weighing my options. It might not even happen yet. I just wanted to run it past you."

"You don't want to come home," she whispered. "I know things aren't great for you right now, but this business was your baby. Remember?"

"I know..." I conceded. "I mean, yes, it was. Back when people didn't want to scalp me or burn me at the stake. But you saw how they were. If I go back there, I'll probably be shutting the doors in a few weeks anyway."

Callie was quiet again, and I knew she knew I was right. She sighed. "Just don't make any rash decisions, Wil."

"I'm not, Cal. That's why I want you to think about it

first. Don't answer me right now, but if I were to offer you the business..." Then I amended, "Well, all property, plant, and equipment anyway." Lord knows there wasn't any goodwill to sell. "I'll call the accountant and get last year's financials, less depreciation. I've got a fair idea, but we should do this properly."

"Wil..."

"If you don't want it or whatever, you can tell me, Cal," I said.

"It's not that," she replied with another sigh. "What will you do?"

"Um, stay here."

"In Key West?"

"Well, yes. But stay here, at the hotel."

There was another beat of silence. Then she asked, "With that other couple?"

"Their names are Adam and Simon," I said. "And yes, they've asked me to stay."

"Jesus Christ, Wil," she cried. "After just two weeks?"

I knew it was rushed. I knew it was fast. "It's... complicated," I offered.

"I bet it is," she huffed.

Then neither of us spoke for a little while. I didn't push her. She had a lot to take in. And so did I.

She sighed again. "It sounds like you've already made up your mind."

I shrugged, though she couldn't see. "What have I got to come home to?"

Her answer was quiet. "Me."

I frowned and swallowed down the lump in my throat. "Cal..."

"I know, I know," she answered. And she did know. Yes,

she was my best friend, and I loved her dearly. But that just wasn't enough, and we both knew it. "What do you want me to say, Wil?"

"I want you to tell me it's okay. To follow my heart. To take a chance at happiness," I answered. "Or I want you to tell me if you think I'm foolish for even considering it, and that you'll pick me up from the airport tomorrow."

She chuckled into the phone. "Yes. I think you're foolish. Fucking crazy, actually. Like you've had too much sun or salt air or something." She let her words hang in the air between us for a long moment, then she sighed again and her voice was softer. "But what kind of friend would I be if I didn't want you to be happy?"

The air left my lungs in a rush. Then I laughed.

"Yeah, be happy, you son of a bitch," she snapped, though I could tell she was smiling. "You listen to me, Wilson Curtis. It better be a damn good offer you're gonna send through to me, Mr. Buy-my-business-or-be-fucking-unemployed. I want a damn good offer."

I was still grinning. "Of course, Cal."

"And one more thing."

"What's that?"

"I want to speak to these two men of yours and set them straight on a few things. I can't be leaving Alabama to kick their asses every time one of them breaks your heart."

I laughed.

She sighed. "Ugh. Fucking hell, Wil."

"I know."

"You're damn lucky I love you."

Her words made me smile. "I know I am. But, Cal?"

She huffed. "What now?"

I chuckled. "I love you too."

I needed to think.

Not about my restaurant, or about finances, or the house. I needed to think about what it was I was entering into—a full-fledged relationship. Not only that, but an already established full-fledged relationship. Adam and Simon knew each other so well. They had a history. They had a *before me*. And I needed to get my head around the whole concept of being in a permanent threesome.

In a *polygamous relationship*.

Fuck.

I *really* needed time to think.

So I did what I'd done every other time I needed to clear my head. I walked barefoot on the beach. I didn't know what it was about the ocean, but it seemed to set things straight in my head. The ebb and flow of the tide was somehow reassuring.

I headed in the direction of the headland with my feet being lapped by the water as I walked. The water was cool and the sun was warm. People smiled as they walked by me. And I walked, and thought, and walked and thought some more.

It'd been a good two hours by the time I got back to the hotel. I'd made some decisions and was starving. The breakfast crew was cleaning up, but I snuck into the kitchen where Syd was packing everything away and pleaded for some fruit salad. She scowled at me, but I batted my eyelashes until she gave in.

She walked out of the cold storage room with a plate of cut fruit and almost handed it over, but held it hostage at the last second. "You're in a better mood today," she quipped. "You actually look like you slept."

I knew she was fishing for information and details on what had happened when she'd left last night. I played along. "Because I did sleep."

Her eyebrows lifted. "Just like how Simon and Adam both look like it was the first time they'd slept in three days. Not to mention they're more pleasant to be around." She smirked at me. "Not a coincidence?"

I smiled at her. "Possibly."

Her smile widened, and she handed over my breakfast. "I'm glad to hear that, Wil."

I walked out, sat at my usual table, and watched the water. When my fruit salad was gone, I made some phone calls. From my accountant back home, I requested full financials for the previous year to be emailed to me ASAP. Then I called the Realtor to get copies of the lease agreement emailed. I ignored the receptionist—a very nosey gossip—and her sly baits for information. Why on earth she didn't just ask outright where I was and why I wanted information on the restaurant's lease, I'll never know. She'd save herself some time.

I knew by the time I hung up that all of Dalton, Alabama, would know Wilson Curtis had called.

I smiled to myself and went in search for Adam and Simon.

I walked through the foyer, past the sign that said Private Only, and went up the stairs. Just as Simon had said, there were two doors. One was closed. The other was wide open, and I could hear them talking.

Adam asked, "Can't you just replace him?"

"Where am I going to find someone to replace him on such short notice? Tonight, Adam. I need someone to work tonight. It's Thursday. That restaurant will be packed."

"What about Wil?"

Simon sighed. "I think we've asked enough of him for one day. I can't ask him to do that."

"Can't ask me to do what?" I asked, moving to stand in the doorway.

Simon looked up, a little shocked, whereas Adam just grinned. He ignored my question and asked his own. "Have you decided?" He was almost bouncing. He had an energy that confounded me.

I looked at him and smiled, but then I shook my head.

Adam's grin died right there and he paled. He swallowed hard and let out a shaky breath. "No, you haven't decided, or no you won't stay?"

I stepped into the room, which I belatedly realized was Simon's office. "I haven't decided. Not really."

Simon turned in his chair to look at me, and I looked at both of them in turn. "I have some questions..."

Adam exhaled and gave me a watery smile. "Of course."

"Well, first off you should know, I, um... I don't have much experience in talking about how I feel or anything like that." I took a deep breath. "This is all very new to me."

Adam took my hand and led me over to Simon's desk. He parked his ass on the edge, so I did the same, and they waited for me to continue.

"And this doesn't mean I've agreed to anything. I'm just trying to get it right in my head first," I clarified. "So I don't want you to get your hopes up"—I looked directly at Adam —"because I haven't made a decision. Yet."

Adam nodded. "I understand."

I knew he'd said he understood, but I worried how he'd react if or when my answer was no. I got the impression Adam didn't handle goodbyes very well at all. I took another deep breath. "I need to know what we'll be. What *we* are to each other, technically." I wasn't being very clear.

Simon blinked, obviously confused. "As in labels?"

I shrugged. "I guess... like if we're out and meet someone, how are we introduced?"

"Well," Adam answered. "If you agreed to stay, we'd be boyfriends. Partners. Like me and Sy are now, only then it would be me and Sy and you."

"You're not really worried about labels, are you?" Simon asked. "What you really want to know is where you fit in?"

My eyes shot to his. "Well, yeah, kinda."

Simon stood up and stepped over to take my hand. "Wil, you would be an equal third. Not a third wheel, not an afterthought. Okay?"

He could read me so well. He knew exactly what I was asking. I gave him a smile. "Okay."

"Wil, this is new to all of us," Simon said with a squeeze of my hand. "Yes, Adam and I have been together as a couple, but not as part of a threesome. It's new for all of us," he said again. "Please don't think you're not included. If we do this, there will be three of us. That's three minds, three sets of opinions, three sets of perspectives. It's going to take some adjusting." Then he brushed the side of my face with his hand. "I think we can do this. Actually, I think we'd be amazing. But, Wil, if you go into this feeling like you're not equal, then we're doomed before we begin." Then his tone brightened. "So to answer your question, yes, I think boyfriends or partners works just fine."

I smiled. "Okay."

Adam smiled at me. "Next question?"

"Well, it's not really a question," I told them. "It's more like a rule."

Adam groaned. "Really? More rules?"

I sighed. "Yes, Adam. Rules." Then I looked between both of them. "I want complete honesty at all times, or it's a deal breaker. I've lied about who I am, and I've been lied to, and I won't do it again."

Simon nodded. "Fair enough. That's not asking for anything I wouldn't. Adam?"

"Oh, sure," he said quickly. "Even if you won't like what I tell you, as long as it's the God's honest truth?"

I nodded. "Yeah, exactly."

Adam smiled. "Like how hideous your shirt is?"

I looked down at my very non-offensive, plain white T-shirt. "What's wrong with it?"

Adam laughed. "Nothing."

Simon sighed. "Adam, this is serious."

"I know," he said, trying not to smile. "I'm just glad it wasn't a rule like that stupid can't-have-sex-when-there's-only-two-of-us rule."

"Oh, I still think that rule should stay," I told them, earning two blank stares.

Adam's head lolled back, and he groaned. "Ugh. Wil. You're trying to kill me."

Simon smiled at Adam, but then he looked at me. "If you'd be more comfortable."

"It's not all about what I want," I replied. "Equal, remember?"

"Fair enough." Simon nodded. "I think that while we're finding our feet in this, we could impose this rule."

Adam sighed. "Well, I could concede maybe a three-month trial, then we can re-evaluate. How does that sound?"

I smiled. "Sounds good."

"But just so I'm clear," Adam said, looking at us both. "The exceptions to that rule were kissing and blow jobs, yes?"

I chuckled. "Yes."

"Good."

"Happy?"

"Yes."

Simon laughed at us. Then he asked, "Any other questions?"

"I have one," Adam said seriously.

Simon and I both looked at him and waited for him to continue.

"Well, I think it's something we need to discuss further, but for right now, I'd like us all to be tested." He looked at us both. "I'm not saying I want to start having unprotected sex. I just think being tested is something we should do." Then he added, "If we're gonna do this whole honesty, full-disclosure thing, that is, then it's a big part of that."

"I agree," I told him. "I have no problems with being tested. In fact, I think it's a very good suggestion."

Simon stepped in front of Adam and kissed his cheek. "I think it's a great idea." Then he smiled at me and seemed pleased at how our discussions had gone. "Anything else you can think of?"

I shrugged. "Only that I better actually see the place I'm going to be living in."

Adam leaped up off the desk, had my hand and was pulling me toward the door before I could blink, and Simon followed with a smile. They led me across the hall to the other door and opened it. It wasn't huge, but it was nice. It had the same type of décor as the rest of the hotel, with dark floors and white walls. The space wasn't big. The furniture was kind of mismatched, but the couch looked comfy. It felt... homey.

"Living room," Adam stated the obvious. "I like to keep it pretty clean and that will probably drive you nuts," he said cheerfully, as he kept pulling me through the room, toward a small kitchenette. "Kitchen. Not as big or as nice as you're used to, I'm sure," Adam said with a shrug. Then he nodded, as though something made sense in his head. "But it's still plenty big enough for you to make me pancakes or eggs."

I laughed, and Simon snorted behind us.

Adam pulled on my hand, leading me down a small hall. "Bathroom in there," he said, pointing to one door. "Bedroom in here," he said, opening the door. "But it's mostly just for clothes and storage and shit." Then he led me to the last door. "Our room," he said.

And I knew he wasn't referring to himself and Simon. When he said *our*, he was referring to me as well.

There was a huge bed, the same as the one in my room downstairs, and a large window which overlooked the court-yard, pool, and the ocean.

"So we'd all sleep in here?" I asked, my voice just a whisper.

Adam smiled, and when I looked back to Simon, he was

leaning against the doorjamb. "Yes, Wil. We'd all sleep in here."

I nodded and let out a somewhat steady breath, in spite of my erratically thumping heart.

Adam squeezed my hand. "So what do you think?"

"It's lovely."

Adam nodded. "It's great, isn't it?" Then he proceeded to ramble on in his enthusiastic way about all the benefits of living there—the laundry service, the cleaners, the people, the view, the ocean.

While Adam talked, Simon walked up beside us and squeezed my arm, silently asking me if I was okay. He must've seen that I was overwhelmed, trying to take it all in. He could see me trying to get my head around it all. Simon was insightful like that. He just kind of knew. I gave him a quick smile to let him know I was okay.

Then my cell phone beeped with an incoming email. It was from the accountant.

Financials attached and cc'd to Ms. Callie Talbot, as requested.

The room had gone quiet, and when I looked up, Simon and Adam were both looking at me. "Just a notification email," I explained. "Callie's been sent the financials on the restaurant."

They both looked a little confused, and it was Simon who clued in first. "She has?"

I nodded. "I asked her if she wanted to buy it."

They both stared, and they both grinned. I turned to Adam and warned him. "It's still in the early stages. The only thing she agreed to was to look over the reports and run some figures. She might not even be able to."

Simon nodded. "And if she can't?"

I looked at him and shrugged. "I don't know. I've had exactly three hours to think about this."

"Then take a week, a month, if you have to," Simon offered. "Stay here, but take the pressure off. Give yourself whatever time you need. We kind of threw you into the deep end, didn't we?"

I chuckled. "Ah, yeah. Kind of."

He smiled. "Sorry."

I stepped closer to him and slid my hand along his jaw, pulling his face closer to mine. "You're not sorry at all," I said, just before I kissed him.

He kissed me slowly. It was the kind of kiss that sends shivers down my spine, and when Adam moved in behind me, I laughed. "Oh, I think we'd better get out of this bedroom."

"Why's that?" Adam asked as he kissed the back of my neck.

"Because that bed's really close, and it looks really big and really, really comfortable."

Simon laughed. "Come on," he said. "Wil's right. If we start now, we'll never get anything done. And I need to get these reports put together." He led us out through the living room and back into his office.

"Is there anything we can do to help?" I asked.

"Ah, it's okay," Simon hedged. "Adam was *helping* me before..."

Adam smiled and nodded, and when I looked back at Simon, he rolled his eyes. I got the impression Adam wasn't *helping* much at all.

I was just about to suggest Adam and I go downstairs and leave Simon alone for a while when my cell phone rang.

I checked the caller ID. It was Callie.

"Hey, Cal."

"Don't you *hey, Cal* me, mister," she said by way of greeting. "Do you have any idea what kind of morning I've had? It's not bad enough that staff call in sick and shit doesn't get done unless you do it yourself, but then you call me and drop a bombshell."

She'd obviously had enough time to think things through, and with the email of financial reports, she now knew I was serious. Adam and Simon were both staring at me, obviously hearing Callie bark at me. I smiled. She not only dealt with stress very well, she thrived.

"You'll handle it just fine, Cal."

"I just wanted you to know I'm having Marta look over the money side of things," she told me. Marta was the local bank branch manager, so I presumed Callie was trying to organize finances.

"Is there anything you need from me?"

"That list is long, Wilson Curtis."

I chuckled, and when Simon said something to Adam, Callie heard it through the phone. "Who's there with you?" Callie asked.

"Um, Adam and Simon are both here with me right now," I said, looking at them. They both stopped talking and stared at me.

"Good," Callie snapped. "*Both*," she mumbled. "Like it's not weird to talk about *both* boyfriends. Anyway, put one of them on the phone. I want to speak to both of them, so it doesn't matter which one goes first."

Oh, shit.

I held my cell phone to my chest and spoke to both Adam and Simon. "Um, you know those really awkward conversations when you get introduced to the friends of new boyfriends and they're all 'you better not hurt him or I'll track you down'?" I looked at both their faces and held my cell phone out to them. "Well, this is going to be one of those conversations. Who wants to go first?"

Simon chuckled, but Adam grinned and bounced over to snatch the phone out of my hand. "Hello," he said brightly. "Adam Preston speaking."

CHAPTER TWELVE

WE COULD HEAR the buzz of Callie's voice as she talked. I almost dreaded to think what she was saying to Adam, but he laughed into the phone, and they started to chat like old friends. He answered *yes*, *no*, and the occasional *absolutely*, but I left him to defend himself and walked over to Simon.

He was standing now, leaning his ass on his desk, and I walked straight up to him, slid my hand along the side of his neck, and kissed him. I spoke in a low voice so only he could hear, "She's trying to sort out money."

He looked at me with hope in his blue eyes and whispered, "Are you staying?"

"I want to. God, I want to." Then I looked over to Adam but whispered to Simon, "But if it can't happen... I don't want to hurt him."

Simon pulled my face back to look at him. "And that right there, Wil, is why I want you to stay."

I gave him a sad smile. "I don't want to hurt you either," I whispered.

Simon didn't say anything. He just kissed me. Slow and

soft, with his hands holding my face, he consumed me. Until Adam spoke beside us. "Well, he's kind of indisposed at the moment," Adam told Callie. "Oh, no, nothing like that. He just has his tongue down Wil's throat."

"Don't tell her that," Simon hissed.

Adam held the phone out to Simon. "She wants to talk to you."

I cringed, and Simon took the phone and cleared his throat. "Simon Stanford speaking."

Adam looked at me and chuckled at Simon's formal manner, and Simon walked over to the window so he could speak to Callie in private. Or be lectured in private, as was probably the case.

Adam pushed me against the desk and kissed me. Hard. The difference between them still surprised me, from Simon's steamy seriousness to Adam's bundle of energy. He pulled back only to grin at me. "Your friend Callie loves me."

I laughed. "Did you dazzle her with your boyish charm?"

"Totally."

I nodded over toward Simon. "Should I be worried about what she's saying to him?"

"Nah," Adam said with a chuckle. Then he kissed me again.

I pulled my face back from his and laughed. Trying to stop Adam from kissing when he wanted to kiss was proving impossible. "Callie wasn't harsh with you?"

He grinned. "Well, she told me if I hurt you, she'd make me the most popular gay guy on the coast by ripping me a second asshole. Does that count?"

I barked out a laugh. "She said that?"

Adam nodded and laughed. "Sure did." Then he

pushed me back onto the desk and pulled my legs around his hips and leaned over me. "Now I have no intention of hurting you, but that second asshole could be useful."

I fell back against the desk so I was lying down and laughed. Adam climbed onto the desk, kneeling over me, and kissed me again, all tongue and open mouth. I tried to pull him closer, to feel his weight on me, but it was difficult given our positions. On a desk.

"Knock that laptop off that desk, you two, and I'm gonna be pissed."

Adam and I stopped kissing and looked over at Simon.

"Sorry, Callie," he said into the phone. "They're... *misbehaving*."

Adam and I both laughed again, and Simon smiled at us. Then he said, "Callie said to stop sounding so damn happy, Wilson Curtis." He laughed quietly at something she said, told her, "I'll be sure to tell him," followed by a goodbye, and he hung up the phone. He walked over to where we were on the desk and slapped Adam's ass. "You need to get ready for work." He handed me my phone. "I need that desk. And Callie said she'd call you later."

Adam climbed off the desk and pulled me to my feet, then lifted my hand to read my watch. "Shit, look at the time." He pecked my lips and told me he'd see me downstairs. He kissed Simon, and as he got to the door, I stopped him.

"Adam, wait!"

He turned at the door and waited for me to talk. So I asked them, "Earlier, when I was walking up the stairs, I heard you both talking. Adam, you said Simon should ask me to do something, and he didn't want to? What was that?"

"Oh, that was nothing," Simon dismissed it quickly.

"That's why I asked while you were both here," I said,

nodding toward Adam, "because I didn't think you'd tell me. Honesty, remember?"

Simon rolled his eyes, and Adam grinned. "Sy thinks it would be unprofessional to ask you to work tonight because you're still *technically* a guest here. And although you've helped out before, he didn't actually *ask* you. He doesn't want you to feel obligated or pressured, but, Wil, I don't mind putting it on ya, you know, with the new honesty policy we have going on," he said, as only he could. "We're really stuck," Adam continued. "We've got the hotel owners in town, a developer throwing money at them, and we can't afford unhappy guests right now."

So Miguel was finished, effective immediately, and they needed a replacement. I looked at Simon, trying to gauge his reaction, or looking for some sort of acknowledgement of what Adam had just said, but he said nothing.

I smiled at him. "I'd love to work tonight for you."

"You'll do it?" Simon asked, clearly surprised and a bit relieved. "Because I haven't even had a chance to look for a replacement. I'm really swamped, and the day's half over and I haven't got anything done. These two really hot guys keep making out on my desk..."

"Of course I'll do it," I said simply. "For you two, I'd do almost anything."

"Anything?" Adam asked with a smirk. "Like move from Alabama to Florida and set up house with two really hot guys?"

I grinned. "I said *almost* anything."

I spent the afternoon packing. Regardless of my decision, I was leaving the hotel room. Not that I'd brought a great deal of stuff, but while both Simon and Adam worked, I sorted, folded, and packed. If I was leaving, I had to be gone by six a.m., so I needed to be organized.

And it was funny how a part of my brain already knew.

I wasn't getting on that plane tomorrow.

As much as I wanted it to be Callie who bought my business, I knew if she couldn't—or wouldn't—it didn't matter.

So I'd take another week like Simon had suggested. Or another month. Or whatever. I'd list it through a realtor, or I'd *give* it to Callie. But I knew my time in Alabama was over.

It wasn't until later that night that I would actually confirmed it though.

I'd seen Sydney while she'd done the lunch shift and told her I was doing the dinner shift. I'd even offered to do extra prep just to fill in time and keep myself occupied while Adam and Simon worked. Needless to say, she hadn't argued.

Dinner had been busy, but I was organized, and the two other kitchen staff and I had handled it easily. And the time had flown. We hadn't seen Simon for the rest of the day, so I'd plated up a steak and salad and had one of the waitstaff deliver it to his office.

But when he still hadn't come down after Adam had closed down the bar, I'd suggested we wait for him in my room. And we'd only been in there less than a minute when my cell phone rang.

I looked at the caller ID, then looked to Adam. "It's Callie." I took a deep breath to steel myself, ready for whatever answer she would give me, and answered her call.

"Hey, Wil," she said sadly, and from her tone alone, my stomach sank to my feet.

"Hey."

I tried to not look at Adam. I knew my tone would speak for itself, he'd see the *no* on my face. But he eased down on the bed slowly, quiet and deflated, and I knew that he knew.

"Well," Callie said. "The bank said it'll be fine."

"What?" I asked, confused. "They what?"

"They said it would be fine," she said again. "Said the figures looked good, actually, and if all you're asking for is product, plant and equipment, it'd be real good buying."

Well, it was a very good business. Until the homophobic town didn't want to catch being gay from the salad.

Adam was staring at me, waiting.

Then Callie said, "But I don't want to say yes."

And my stomach twisted. My voice was quiet. "Why not?"

"Because if I say yes, then you won't come home."

"Cal," I said. "It's okay. If you can't do it..."

Adam fell back so he was lying on the bed with his feet still on the floor. He put his hands over his face.

Before I could tell him it would be okay, Callie spoke in my ear, "Please tell me why the hell I'm going to miss you so much?" she cried. "You've given me stress lines today, gray hair too, probably."

I climbed up onto the bed and sat cross-legged next to Adam. I pulled one of his hands away from his face and held it, but his eyes stayed closed.

"Wil, are you there?" Callie asked.

"Yeah, I'm here." My voice was quiet, even to my own ears.

After a long moment's silence, she sighed. "How am I

supposed to do this without you? It's always been us, Wil. You and me."

And she wasn't just talking about the restaurant.

I nodded, and my voice was just a whisper when I answered, "I know, Cal."

"Goddammit, Wil. I want you to be happy." I heard some voices in the background, then Cal's muffled voice as she spoke to them. It sounded as if she was giving orders. "Sorry about that," she said to me. "Just doing inventory."

I looked at my watch. "At eleven at night?"

"Well, I needed to do an inventory count because I just bought the goddamn business, didn't I?"

It was surprising I didn't laugh out loud. But I just nodded in relief and blinked back tears instead. It was like one of those defining moments when the pieces just simply fell into place.

"Thank you, Callie."

She told me she loved me, and she'd speak to me tomorrow to sort out details of the contract. Then she told me she'd better get going, because at this rate, she'd be counting fucking spoons and forks until morning. Then I was smiling at a dial tone.

I squeezed Adam's hand, and with such sad eyes, he looked at me. But then he looked at my smile, and his eyes went wide.

"Yes?"

I nodded. "Yes."

And in a flash, he leaped up and tackled me back onto the bed, pinning me down with his hands. His grin was beautiful. "Really? You're staying? For real?"

I laughed and nodded. "I am."

He kissed me quickly. And he stared at me for a long moment, then he kissed me slowly. He pecked my lips again and again, and when he pulled away, he climbed off me and pulled me up. "We need to go tell Sy."

We knocked on his office door and got a tired, "Yeah," in response.

Adam opened the door, and a worn-out-looking Simon glanced up from his paperwork. He looked at our joined hands and happy faces, and he smiled. "I just finished up," he told us. He walked over, and Adam quickly wrapped his free hand around him and pulled him into a three-way hug.

Simon was drained. He kind of slumped into us and sighed. "I'm really sorry," he said. "It's not how I wanted to spend Wil's last day here." Then he added, "If it's his last day here."

"It's not," Adam said, grinning.

Simon's head shot up, and he looked at me with wide blue eyes. "It's not?" he asked. "You're not leaving?"

I shook my head. "Callie just called. She got a loan pre-approval and—"

My words were cut off by Simon's lips on mine. His hands were suddenly in my hair, touching and gripping, holding my face to his while he kissed me. We both moaned and when Adam whimpered beside us, Simon broke our kiss, only to rest his forehead on mine. "Oh, Wil. Thank you."

Then Simon kissed Adam, then Adam kissed me, and the three of us were a kissing, groping, panting mess until Adam said, "Bed. Now."

But we didn't go downstairs to my room. We went across the hall into the apartment.

The apartment where I now lived.

We stumbled to the bedroom, trying to undress but not wanting to stop kissing. Our hands never left each other, our mouths always touching some of us. We were on the bed, the three of us writhing hard, and grinding, seeking, needing.

I ended up riding Adam, sinking down on his cock while Simon took me in his mouth. Such dual sensations, such pure pleasure. Adam filled me so completely, brushing my gland with every thrust, and no sooner did I shoot down Simon's throat than Adam flexed underneath me, stilled, and with a strangled cry, he pulsed inside me.

And when I thought my body had had enough, Simon flipped me onto my back, folded my legs up near my chest, and slid inside me.

I groaned, long and low, and my still-hard cock throbbed. I wondered if my body would ever have enough, if I'd ever have enough. When I came again and still wanted more, I doubted I ever would.

———

It was well after midnight when we showered together, and when we walked back into the bedroom, it was different. Still great, but just different. There was no unbridled passion pushing us onto the bed. This time Adam climbed up and sat in the middle, and Simon walked around to the side near the window while I stood at the door. Adam looked at me and smiled like he always did as he patted the bed beside him. "Your side," he said.

I climbed up beside him and tried not to grin. Simon was now sitting on his side and they were both smiling at me. I burst out laughing. The happiness just bubbled out. Adam laughed and Simon shook his head, but we all lay down, snuggled into each other, each of us touching the others, and fell asleep.

———

The next morning, I woke up in a strange room. The light was different, the bed was different, but the smell was familiar—as were the arms around me.

Adam's nose traced circles on the back of my neck. "Aren't you going swimming?" I asked, my voice croaking with sleep.

He kissed my shoulder with smiling lips. "Mm-mm." He shook his head. "Not today."

Without rolling over—or even turning my head—I reached behind me, blindly searching for Simon. He took my hand. "I'm here."

I sighed, more content than I had ever been.

"It's six-thirty," Simon said. "Your plane to Alabama would be leaving right about now."

I squeezed his hand, and Adam's arm tightened around me, and I told them without an ounce of doubt something I felt in my bones. In my heart. "There's nowhere else I'd rather be."

CHAPTER THIRTEEN

WE REALLY NEEDED TO TALK. So much had happened so fast, and because we were now technically a threesome, we *really* needed to talk.

So I collected my bag from my old room, Adam went downstairs and collected some coffee and fruit salad for the three of us, and Simon checked his emails. Then for the rest of the morning, that was what we did.

We sat in the apartment and talked.

I told them I'd spoken to Dee, and whether it was right or wrong, she'd told me a little about their families. I took Adam's hand and told him I knew his parents had kicked him out when he was just seventeen.

He nodded and sighed. "Yeah. It wasn't always easy," he said dismissively. Then he brightened. "Simon always shakes his head at me, and he thinks I'm a little OCD about the apartment. I usually spend most of my time cleaning it, making sure everything's in the right place." Adam looked at me then and gave me a sad smile. "I'll probably annoy you and drive you crazy, but I just like to make sure it's a nice place to live, ya know? Because I didn't always have that."

I nodded slowly. I thought I understood. "Were some of the places you stayed not very nice?"

Simon rubbed Adam's back, and Adam shrugged. "Not really very nice, no. And I know what it's like to have nothing." He took a deep breath. "I know what it's like to not have a home, and now that I have one, I want to make sure it's clean and homey..." His words trailed off as he looked around the room. "That probably doesn't make any sense to you."

I squeezed his hand. "It makes perfect sense, Adam."

He threaded our fingers. Simon kissed his cheek, and Adam gave him a smile, then he sighed again. "When I left New York, I didn't have very much. Did you know it's cheaper to pay for an overnight ticket on a Greyhound bus than it is to pay for a night in a motel?"

I shook my head. I hadn't known.

"I just ended up going south, as far south as I could," Adam explained. "I ended up here in Key West. Even though I was underage, I talked my way into a job picking up glasses and stocking fridges at a local bar. Told them I didn't want money, just some food, maybe a bed."

Oh, fuck. My stomach somersaulted to the floor.

Adam looked far off and I could see he was remembering that time in his life. "I could've easily fallen into the drug scene. Lots of the kids I ran with did. Some hooked for it." Adam shook his head, as though he was shaking off a bad memory. Then he looked at me and asked, "Wanna know what I did every day?"

I nodded.

"I swam," he said. "I used to be in a swim club back home, trained every day. So it was nice to have something familiar, ya know?" He smiled. "Plus, the water was right there, and it didn't cost me any money to swim in the ocean."

"Oh, Jesus," I whispered. "I'm sorry."

While I blinked back tears, he smiled his usual smile. "Don't be sad, Wil. Because not long after that I was taken in by a batshit-crazy black woman from Barbados, who introduced me to Sy."

Dee. Dee had taken him in.

Adam laughed. "She felt sorry for me and fed me. I offered to wash up at the café for her trouble, and she stood there with her hand on her hip and pointed her finger at me." Then Adam mocked her perfectly. "'Young man, you will be here at eleven a.m. sharp every morning. You'll wash up and clean and do whatever the hell it is I tell you to do. You will come home with me and get cleaned up, young man. I have a spare room and a seat at my dinner table that'll cost you a week's work.'"

I smiled at his impersonation of Dee.

"So that's what I did," he said with a shrug. "She fed me and gave me a bed, and I gave her free labor. It was the sweetest deal I'd had."

"But then you met Simon?" I asked, looking at Simon, who'd been quiet to let Adam tell his story.

Adam nodded. "He was seeing some other guy—who was a loser, by the way," Adam said with a serious nod. "But he was taking over as hotel manager and needed a bartender."

Simon chuckled. "He was smitten."

"I totally was," Adam laughed and nodded without shame. "Here was this gorgeous and smart guy who needed someone to tend bar. There was no way I was letting *that* pass me by. So when Sy asked if I'd worked in a bar before, I said yes."

"You lied," Simon said with a smile.

Adam chuckled. "Technically picking up glasses and stocking fridges in a bar isn't what he meant." I laughed at them. Simon pulled Adam's chin around to face him and kissed him.

Then Simon told me about his family. "Not much to tell really," he started out. "Mom and Dad are still together. Got a brother, Jamie, and a sister, Rachel, both older than me, and they both work for Dad. He has an import-export business." Then Simon shrugged. "I guess I got off pretty lucky. Jamie and Rachel were both willing to make Dad happy by working for him, and both of them will make Mom happy by giving them grandchildren. So there were few expectations on me."

"But they know you're gay?" I asked.

"Oh, sure," he answered. "I told them when I was about fifteen. Well," he amended, "Jamie told them when I was about fifteen. They weren't exactly happy about it, but all things considered, they took it very well."

I nodded. Compared to Adam, I guess they had.

"Did your parents know?" Adam asked. "You know, before they died?"

I shook my head. "I'd like to think they would have accepted me being gay, but the truth is, I doubt they would have. I know they'd have kicked me out, cut me off, whatever," I said, and Adam squeezed my hand. "It's easier to dream of how I'd have liked them to react now that they're gone and I know it can't ever be proven otherwise. So in my mind, I see them being loving and supportive, whereas the honest truth is it wouldn't have been like that at all."

"And they died two years ago?" Simon asked gently.

I nodded. "It was a car accident. We lived on a few acres, and they were driving to town. There was an oncoming truck that crossed lanes." I didn't need to fill in the rest. I sighed. "Rod was one of the cops who came to tell me. Then he came back later on to check on me." I shook my head as I remembered. "You know, I had no idea he was gay. To be honest, I don't think he knew he was gay," I said with a laugh. Then I exhaled. "But I was upset and he put his arms around me. Nothing happened then, but the way he held me wasn't exactly a professional pat on the back. And over the next few weeks, he would stop by to see how I was doing, and he'd touch my arm or shoulder a little longer than normal."

"And that's how things started between you?" Adam asked.

I nodded. "In all the time we were together, we never talked about what we did. It was like our dirty little secret."

"Did you love him?" Simon asked. "Do you still love him?"

I looked at both of them and answered honestly, "I thought I did." I shook my head. "But then I met you two..."

Adam grinned. "See? I knew you had feelings for us!"

I laughed, embarrassed. "I'm here, aren't I?"

"Well, yes," Adam answered. "And you know how we feel about you?"

I nodded, feeling myself blush.

Adam traced his fingers over my warmed cheek. "And the fact you're here, the fact you're now living with us, tells us you feel the same, even if you can't say it."

I swallowed loudly and looked at them. "This all happened so quickly, didn't it?"

"We can make this work, Wil," Simon said. "I know there will be some growing pains, but I have no doubt the three of us can do this."

I nodded and gave them a weak smile. "But living and working together, it's gonna be pretty full-on."

Adam smirked at me. "It's gonna be awesome!"

I couldn't help but chuckle, and Simon leaned over and kissed me. "I know you're worried about that, but with us all working different shifts and odd hours, you might be surprised at how often we're not together."

"True," I conceded. "Oh, I guess we should talk terms of employment."

So we did. Simon and I discussed the ins and outs of what we both expected, while Adam snuggled in between us. We talked rates and hours, responsibilities and contracts, and when Adam started to fidget, we knew he'd gotten bored.

He started to rub his hand over his dick, and grinned without shame. "I can't help it!" he defended himself. "I can't be lying here in between both of you for this long without someone getting off. Figured it may as well be me."

Simon chuckled, and I snorted out a laugh. He was incorrigible. Absolutely, adorably incorrigible.

Adam just kept on grinning, then sat up on the back of the sofa between us, undid the fly of his cargos, and pulled his hardening cock out. "Wanna share?"

So Simon and I both leaned in and took turns giving him head, then at the same time, we kissed each other around his cock. We tongued his shaft, his balls, and the head while sucking on each other's tongues and lips. Our mouths never stopped working him over.

"Oh fuck!" Adam cried. "Yeah, both of you. Kiss my cock like that."

And when Adam started to thrust into our mouths, Simon got up on his knees and took the length of Adam's cock in his mouth. I watched as he took him in and swallowed him as Adam flexed and cried out as he came.

I grabbed Adam so he didn't fall backward and slid him down onto the sofa with us. He was a moaning, boneless mess, and when I turned to look at Simon, his eyes were dark. Ignoring a blissed-out Adam, Simon pounced on me, pushing me back down on the sofa and thrusting his tongue into my mouth. All I could taste was Adam.

I wrapped my arms around him and tried to open my legs for him, but with Adam still at one end, the sofa was too small. "Need a bigger sofa," I panted as Simon kissed down my neck.

Adam chuckled and squeezed his way out from underneath us, giving us the entire couch to ourselves. I wriggled underneath Simon so his weight settled on me completely and bucked my hips into his. He kissed me like he couldn't get enough of me.

Then Adam was back, wearing his work uniform. "Remember, no fucking without me."

We stopped kissing to look at him. He was grinning at us, almost like he was daring us. So Simon maneuvered us into a sixty-nine position. I undid his fly and exposed his long, hard cock and swiped it with my tongue, while he did the same to me.

Adam groaned out a chuckle as he walked to the door. "Save some for me."

The next two weeks were like living in a fairy tale. Life with Simon and Adam couldn't have been better while we were still getting to know one another inside and outside of the bedroom. I ran with Simon in the morning and we'd have breakfast, then I'd spend a few hours with Adam before we started work. It was a busy two weeks, but it was also the most relaxed I ever remembered being.

I'd sorted out shifts and duties with Syd, and between us we had the restaurant running like a well-oiled machine. We laughed while we worked, and even the other staff said they now looked forward to coming in, which was a far cry from how it had been with Miguel.

I spoke to Callie every day. She was doing well, as was the restaurant, and I missed her like crazy. But I needed to go back to Alabama to finalize the sale of the restaurant. I could've had a lawyer organize it for me down here, but I figured I'd need to organize my house and collect a few things. I'd only come here with one suitcase. So I'd scheduled time with Syd to make sure the shifts were covered and booked my ticket.

Simon and Adam both understood why I had to go back, and although they were concerned, they agreed I should go. So I was surprised when Simon called my cell, telling me to come up to the apartment. He sounded worried, and the fact I was only downstairs in the kitchen and he hadn't come down to get me had me concerned.

I raced upstairs to find Simon trying to calm down a rather agitated Adam. My heart leaped to my throat. "What's wrong?"

Adam stood up and looked at me. He looked like he was about to be sick, or maybe he was having a panic attack or something. And he was holding my plane ticket in his hand. "I was tidying up and found this. I wasn't snooping," he said. "You left it on the counter."

"Adam, please, tell me what's wrong."

He held up my plane ticket. "This is one way, Wil. One fucking way! When were you going to tell us?"

I didn't understand. "Tell you what?"

"That you weren't coming back!" he yelled, tears filling his eyes. "Fucking hell, Wil." His voice cracked. He could hardly speak. "We finally find you. We fall in love with you. And you do this." He held up the ticket.

I crossed the floor quickly and took his face in my hands. "I'm not leaving you, baby."

He shook his head and his tears spilled down his cheeks. If my heart hadn't been hammering so hard, I'm sure it would have broken in my chest. I pulled him against me. "Adam, baby, it's a one-way ticket because I'm driving my car back. Remember? I told you I had a car that I'd need to bring back, and I figured I'd be bringing back more clothes and other personal stuff, so it made sense to fly up and drive back. I told you this, didn't I?"

Adam shook his head against me. "You told me about the car," he whispered. "But you never said you were driving it back this time, and when I found the one-way ticket, I didn't even think..."

Fuck.

"You told me," Simon murmured.

I looked over to Simon and tightened my arms around Adam. "I'm so sorry, baby," I whispered into his neck. "I didn't mean to *not* tell you. I didn't mean to scare you."

Adam's arms tightened around me, his fingers dug into my sides, and he nodded. I looked over to Simon again and motioned with my hand for him to come over to us, and we both held on to Adam until he felt better. I realized right there just how ingrained Adam's fear of his loved ones leaving him really was—courtesy of his parents—and I swore to myself and to both Adam and Simon I'd never make the same mistake again.

We added another rule that day. Open communication on every fucking thing.

It wasn't that the fairy tale ended that day. It just made this relationship real. It wasn't a game. It wasn't a holiday fling. It was real. Real hearts on the line, real love at stake.

And later that night when the three of us were in bed, just two weeks after officially moving there, I told them I loved them for the very first time. And the next day at the airport as I was about to board the plane, I told them again.

Simon told me later that Adam just beamed the entire day.

CHAPTER FOURTEEN

GOING BACK to Alabama was strange. I sat in the taxi on the ride from the airport to my parents' house and stared out of the window. The passing countryside was so familiar, yet something was different. And by the time we'd pulled into the well-known drive a few miles out of Dalton, I knew what was off.

The countryside hadn't changed at all.

I had.

This town wasn't my home anymore. It wasn't where I belonged. It never had been.

Walking into my parents' house was always a little off-putting. It was *their* house. Sure, it was the house I'd grown up in. It was familiar, but since my parents had died, it had never really felt like home. It was too big, too quiet, too not-me. I mean, I still slept in my childhood bedroom because it felt bizarre to take the master suite. Because that was Mom and Dad's room, not mine.

It just didn't feel like home anymore because they weren't in it.

When I thought of home, I thought of a small apartment with a king-sized bed. I thought of two guys, one with black hair, one with blond, how they smelled, how they laughed, and how they made me feel.

That was where my home was.

But I had a list of things to do and a list of people to see in Dalton. And first on that list was Callie.

It was a little after ten a.m., so I knew she'd be at work, getting things organized for the day. I walked through the very familiar service doors and called out, "Callie?"

She stuck her head out from the dry storage area and squealed. Then she ran and threw her arms around me. "Oh my God," she cried as she hugged me. "I've missed you!" Then she pulled back, and looked me over. "Holy shit, you look so good!"

I grinned at her, dismissing her compliment, but she stared at me.

"No, Wil, I mean it," she said with something like wonder in her eyes. "You've had some sun, and you look like you lost a few pounds. Jesus, Wil. What's it been, three or four weeks? You look..." She shook her head.

"Running every day on the beach and eating fruit and salads will do that."

"No." She shook her head. "Oh my God, Wilson Curtis, you're in love."

I felt myself blush. I nodded. "Oh, Callie, they're just wonderful."

Her eyes got teary. But then she turned and walked over to the coffee machine, poured two cups, and moved to a table, which meant we were about to talk.

"How's it all going?" I asked as we sat down. "Things been okay? I presume business is back to good?"

"We can talk about work in a bit," she said, sipping her coffee. "First I want to talk about these two men of yours."

I sipped my coffee, wondering where to start. "Well, Adam's the wild one. He's always smiling and could charm the leg off a chair. Simon's more reserved, quieter, but he's funny and so smart." I pulled my phone out of my pocket and scrolled through some photos and showed the screen to Callie. "Here they are. Simon's the dark-haired one. Adam's the blond."

She looked at the screen, at the picture of the three of us with our arms around each other, smiling for Sydney to take the photo. Then she looked at me. "So how does the three-guy thing work?"

I'd known this was coming. I tried not to get defensive. "I don't know exactly. It just does. It's like we're a puzzle that needed three pieces." I shrugged. I didn't know how to explain it any better than that.

Callie thought about that for a while. "And no one gets left out?"

I shook my head. "It's the opposite of that, if that makes sense. It's like there's... more."

Callie looked at me and her brow creased. "Wil, you spent two years with that asshole Rod, and I just don't want you to go from one relationship where your needs weren't met to another one. There's merit to the saying 'three's a crowd,' Wil. Doesn't one of you feel left out at some point?"

"That's just the point, Cal. Even without the hiding and secrecy I went through, I'm getting double what I ever had with Rod. Double what I could have ever had with him. It's double the attention, double the conversation, double the emotion. Double everything."

"Double the heartache."

"I won't justify this to you," I said gently. "You don't have to like it. But I'm *with* them. Both of them. I can't explain it, Cal. I can't describe how this works—it just does.

We work. We each contribute something. We're like three pieces that just fit."

Callie sighed, then was silent for a while. "I can see you're happy. Jesus, you've never looked so happy. But are you sure this is what you want? It's not some rebound thing? An extended vacation fling?"

"It's more than that. So much more than that. Come back with me, meet them."

Callie rolled her eyes at the suggestion. "How can I? I just bought a business!"

I chuckled and conceded a nod. "True." And our talk of my decision to enter a polygamous relationship was over. I knew she'd be concerned, but as long as she knew I was happy, she'd be happy. "So, let's discuss this business-buying adventure."

So we did. But I left before the lunchtime rush started, not wanting to be seen by anyone, paid my lawyer a visit, then went back to the house. The fewer people who knew I was back, even for a day or so, the better. Later that night, Callie came by with two bottles of wine and helped me finish packing.

Though we didn't get much packing done, we drank, we laughed, and we cried. So many memories. Although it wasn't really a goodbye, we both knew it kind of was. And while she slept soundly in the bed down the hall, I stared at the ceiling. This house was just a house to me. Sure, I had memories of my childhood here, memories of my parents. But that was all they were. Memories.

The next morning, I packed a few things into my car, hugged Callie until she couldn't breathe, and stopped in to see the real estate agent before I left. I walked out of the office onto the sidewalk, pulled out my phone, opened the contacts, and hit the first number.

Simon answered. "Hey, you."

"Hey," I said. Even the sound of his voice made me happy. "Can you do me a favor? Tell Adam I'm coming home a day early."

I swear I could hear him smile. "You are?"

"Yeah," I sighed. "There's nothing for me here."

He told me he loved me, to drive safe, and that he'd see me soon. I was grinning as I got to my car, when I saw Rod frozen on the sidewalk. He was staring at me.

I looked at him for a long second, and if I'd expected to feel something, anything, I didn't.

Nothing.

He looked... shocked. I didn't speak to him, I didn't smile or wave, nothing. I simply got in my car and headed home.

Home.

Back to Florida, back to Adam and Simon.

Almost fourteen hours later, I got there. Even as tired as I was, I was excited when I pulled up at the hotel. I left my stuff in the car and went straight inside. I headed directly to the bar where I knew Adam would be, and he grinned his heart-stopping grin when he saw me. Then he walked out to meet me and kissed me so damn thoroughly we even got whistles and applause from the guests.

He pulled his mouth from mine and smirked. Then he looked over my shoulder and his eyes softened. I followed his gaze to find a smiling Simon standing near the foyer, watching us. So I walked to him and kissed him, just like Adam had kissed me.

And later that night, after the first round of blow jobs, I told them all about my trip. I told them how I'd met with Callie, how I'd gotten drunk with Callie, and how I'd run into Rod on the street.

Then I told them of my decision to sell my parents' house. They were surprised, to say the least, but I reassured them that going back had only reinforced how much leaving was the right thing to do. I'd asked the real estate agent to organize a moving company to put the furniture into storage and to send me the paperwork. I told them Alabama wasn't home for me anymore.

Then I asked them to DP me.

I'd seen double penetrations done in porn, and I always wondered what would make a guy *want* to have two cocks in his ass at the same time. Now I knew.

I wanted to feel owned. I wanted both of them inside me at the same time. I wanted to feel both of them moving inside me. I wanted them to have me like that. I needed it.

Simon orchestrated it, taking extra care to prep me longer, stretch me farther, and by the time I was already impaled on Adam's cock, I was almost begging for Simon to join in. So he did, pushing into my already breached hole. It stretched and burned like nothing I'd ever felt. Adam started to pant, and Simon started to groan.

And I started to float.

It was heavenly. I was so full of them, so completely and thoroughly theirs.

It was perfect.

That night I slept in Adam's spot, with their arms wrapped tightly around me.

That was the first time Adam didn't sleep in the middle.

The second time was the very next night. Only this time it was Simon who lay between us.

He'd been kinda quiet after they'd DPed me. Even the next night while the three of us were lounging on the sofa after work, he kept asking me if I was okay, if I was hurt or sore. The more I thought about it, the more I realized he *always* asked if we were okay. He always fussed over us if we'd bottomed, making sure we were fine.

I reassured him I was more than fine. A pleasant ache was how I described it. But he didn't seem too convinced. "Kinda like a first time," I hedged, trying to explain it.

Simon didn't speak for a while, and I took his silence to mean he understood what I meant. But then he said, "My first time was... um..." He swallowed hard. It wasn't like him to be so unsure.

My heart tightened in my chest at his words, and Adam sat up to look at him. "Sy?"

He swallowed. "I, um... I, uh..." He scrubbed his hand over his face and through his hair. "My first time," he whispered. "He hurt me. I was young, just sixteen, and I wasn't really ready, and he, well, he... he hurt me."

"Oh, baby," Adam whispered.

I clicked the television off. "Oh, Simon."

"I've been too scared to bottom since," he said.

"That's okay, Sy," Adam told him. "A lot of guys don't do it."

Simon swallowed thickly and whispered, "I think I want to." Then he looked up at us. "I see how much pleasure it can be for you, and then last night, Wil, when we were both inside you..." He shook his head and stared at me. "God, what you gave us last night was a gift. I've never..." He sighed deeply. "I want to share that with both of you."

Adam and I stared at him. Then Simon's eyes went

wide as he realized what he said. "Not the DP!" he barked out. "I don't know if I'll ever be ready for that, but... but I think I want to try bottoming."

I took his hand and gave it a squeeze. "You *think* you want to try?"

He looked at me, and with a little more conviction, he said, "I want to."

I knew this was huge. This was uncharted territory.

Simon ducked his head, so I knelt in front of him and cupped his face in my hands, making him look at me. "Are you sure?"

His eyes widened and glistened, but he nodded.

Oh, Simon...

Keeping his face in my hands, I kissed him. I kissed his face, his closed eyelids, his mouth, his jaw. Then Adam took Simon's face in his hands and kissed him sweetly. "Sy, baby, we'll take care of you."

And I realized he wouldn't be the one in charge like he usually was. Simon was going to need someone to direct this, to show him how it would happen, to show him he'd be okay. Then remembering our first time together and the words he'd said to me, I repeated them back to him.

"This is how we're going to do this," I told him, his face still close to mine. "You're going to fuck Adam while I fuck you."

Simon exhaled in a rush and nodded, relieved. I pulled him to his feet and led us to the bedroom. We stood at the foot of the bed, in a close triangle, and I pulled Simon against us both. "We won't hurt you. We could never hurt you."

He looked at us and nodded. "I want this. I want to have this with both of you. I want it to be with both of you."

Adam got the buttons of Simon's shirt undone and

peeled it back off his shoulders, letting it fall to the floor. In undressing each other, there was never a moment when four hands weren't on him, two mouths, two bodies.

Not long after, Adam lay on his back in the middle of the bed, with his knees up near his chest. Simon was over him, fully seated inside him. I'd taken my time prepping Simon with my tongue and my fingers until he was moaning and begging, and when I finally pressed against his ready hole, I stopped.

Leaning over his back, I kissed his shoulder and whispered, "Are you sure?"

He nodded and exhaled sharply. Adam cupped his face and held him while I pushed inside. He was so tight. Fuck, he was tight. But I went as slowly as my body would allow, and soon set the rhythm. Adam never let go of Simon's face, holding him, kissing him, while I knelt behind them, fucking them both.

I'd never experienced anything like it.

Being inside Simon was amazing, but being his first in a long time, having him trust me, love me enough to do it, was the real gift. I took my time, measuring his breaths, his sounds, rubbing my hands over his back, kissing where I could reach. I was buried inside him as far as I could go, and I rocked into him while he rocked into Adam. When I was sure he was okay, I pushed a little harder.

"Adam, fuck his mouth with your tongue," I said with a grunt. Adam pulled Simon's face to his. All I could see was Adam's hands in Simon's hair.

And Simon started to make sounds like I'd never heard from him. It was a groan and a cry and a whimper, all rolled into one. So I pushed a little harder, pushing him farther into Adam, and he moaned with pleasure, so I did it again and again and again until he came.

God, he came so hard.

Adam cried out, flexing into Simon, taking Simon's pulsing cock deeper while his own orgasm spilled between them. I followed a few thrusts later.

We lay in a heap of sated limbs until I got out of bed to clean us up. After I'd washed them down with a warm, wet cloth, I crawled onto the bed on the other side of Simon and wrapped him up between us.

I kissed his temple. "Sy, baby, you okay?"

"Yeah, I am," he murmured with a sleepy smile. "That was... great." He snuggled in-between us. "Love you," he said to both of us.

Adam and I both kissed the sides of his head, and we answered him together. "Love you, too."

Simon never said anything else that night. He just held tightly onto both of us, and when he'd fallen asleep, Adam leaned his head on his bent arm to look at me. He murmured, "I don't think I could love either of you any more than I do right now."

I reached out and touched his face. "Me too, baby. Me too."

And I didn't think it would get any better than that.

I didn't know how it possibly could.

And it was only two days later that it all fell to shit.

CHAPTER FIFTEEN

IT WAS mid-afternoon before the dinner shift, and I was behind the bar helping Adam cut up his fruit garnishes. And when I say *helping* Adam, I mean doing it all for him. Not that I minded. He was being his usual charming self to some guests at the bar, telling them tales of nights out clubbing and making them laugh.

Four people walked in through the entrance doors, through the foyer, and toward the paved courtyard area by the pool, talking amongst themselves and looking around curiously. I recognized the two women. They were the owners of the hotel, but I had no clue as to who was with them.

Adam stopped talking. He left the other guys mid-conversation and stepped up beside me. "Can you go get Sy?"

I looked at him. It wasn't very often he was this serious. "Sure," I told him. Then I looked at the two strange men. "Why? Who are they?"

"I don't know who the guy is in the black suit is, but that guy in the gray suit?" Adam gave a pointed glance to the middle-aged man wearing the expensive gray suit. "That's Hartley."

Hartley. The developer who had made it his mission in life to rid the Gulf coast of gay people. That Hartley. Was standing in the hotel. *Our* hotel.

I raced upstairs, and even though the office door was open, I called out anyway. "Sy?"

Simon spun around to see me. "What's up?"

"The owners are downstairs," I told him quickly. "There're two men with them. Adam said one of them is that Hartley guy."

Simon stood, grabbed his jacket off the back of his chair, and with a mumbled "Fuck" he went downstairs. I followed him, of course, but as he walked up to the owners and the two suited men, I returned to the bar.

I heard them make introductions, but from where Adam and I stood, we could hear little else. We just watched them. I was no expert in body language, but I could tell from Simon's stance it didn't look good.

But just a few minutes later, the meeting disbanded. The two older women left, and Simon stalked over to us, leaving Hartley and his suited friend, who I assumed was either a financial or a legal adviser, standing in the open courtyard.

Simon walked in behind the bar and stood between us. He spoke in whispered tones, through gritted teeth, "They're just here to look around, apparently." He shook his head. "The owners wanted to introduce him to me, so I was aware of who he was and why he was here."

A wide-eyed Adam looked at Simon. "Why is he here, Sy?"

It was very obvious why Hartley was here, but I guessed Adam needed to hear it. Simon stepped closer to Adam and put his hand on Adam's arm. "They're negotiating prices. Hartley's buying the hotel."

Adam looked at Simon, then to me, then back to Simon, and he shook his head. "What does that mean?" He looked around at the hotel and the guests at the tables, in the pool. "I mean, what does that mean for this place? For us? Where does that leave us?"

Before Simon or I could answer him, Hartley and his advisor walked over to the bar. "Simon, isn't it?"

Simon answered coldly, "Yes."

"We'll just be heading off," Hartley said with a sniff. Then he looked around at the couple kissing in the pool and the couple at one of the tables. He almost sneered. "I think I've seen enough."

Simon gave him a nod, but when Hartley turned to leave, Simon called out, "Can I ask you a question?"

Hartley gave him a sly smile. "Sure."

"What are your plans for this place?"

Hartley shrugged, like it made no difference. "I'll knock it down." He looked around at the all-male couples. "Build something more to my standards."

I couldn't believe it. The audacity of that arrogant, homophobic piece of shit left me speechless. The three of us watched him leave in silence, and when I turned to look at Simon, he was looking at Adam.

Adam's voice was quiet, distant. "Sy?"

"It'll be okay, Adam," Simon answered, putting his hand on Adam's hip. "It'll be okay, babe." But when Simon looked back at me, he didn't look like it was going to be okay at all.

I didn't know what to say. What could I say? I'd only been here for a month and now I was facing the same goddamn issues that had plagued me in Alabama. I didn't know what we were going to do. The hotel was being sold out from under us, and worse still, sold to a homophobe who had more money than he had tolerance.

Where would we live? Where would we work?

I looked at Simon. I knew he was putting on a brave face for Adam. He was always protective of Adam, and rightly so. Adam hadn't had it easy, and the thought of being unemployed and homeless once more must have terrified him.

"We'll talk about it later," Simon said soothingly. "After work tonight, okay? I'll go upstairs, make some phone calls, and see what I can find out."

Adam nodded, and ever the professional, went back to serving the guys seated at the bar. He smiled for them, but it was hardly genuine. The guests didn't notice, but Simon and I certainly did.

We went about our usual work, but there were no jokes between the bar and kitchen, no silly comments, no sexy remarks. And at the end of the night, when Adam and I went upstairs to the apartment, Simon was already there.

He told us how the owners hadn't even considered selling until Hartley approached them. They knew of his reputation, they knew of his reasons for wanting the hotel, and although they didn't like the man personally, his offer was good.

"That's a fucking cop-out," I said through gritted teeth. My uncertainty had crept into anger, and my tone clearly surprised both of them. "That Hartley's a homophobic prick!"

Adam and Simon stared at me, wide-eyed at my outburst. It wasn't like me to be so angry, but it was happening again. A-fucking-gain. I was about to have another business ripped away from me because of close-minded, hateful assholes. I looked at Simon and told him, "We have to do something!"

"Like what, Wil?" he cried. His tone matched mine. "What the fuck am I supposed to do?"

"Something!" I yelled back at him. "Something! Anything!"

Adam looked back and forth between us. He looked scared, and he whispered, "Please don't fight."

I sighed and ran my hands through my hair. "We're not fighting, Adam baby," I said softly. "We're just..." I wasn't sure what to call it.

"Yelling at each other," Adam filled in for me.

Simon walked over to Adam and wrapped one hand around his neck and pulled him in for a hard hug. "We're not fighting, baby. We didn't mean to yell."

I walked over to them and slid my hand along Simon's jaw. "I'm sorry I yelled," I told him sincerely. "I was upset and angry, but not at you. It was misdirected, and I'm sorry."

Simon kissed the heel of my hand.

"What will we do?" Adam asked.

Simon pulled away from Adam so he could look at him square on. "Babe, you know I love it here, and I don't want to leave either. But no matter what, no matter where we are"—Simon looked up at me as well—"no matter where we are, we'll all be together, okay?"

Adam nodded. "I know, it's just... well, it's our home."

I shook my head. "No."

Both Adam and Simon stared at me. "What?"

"We stay. We fight this Hartley guy."

Simon looked at me as though I'd lost my mind. "How?"

"I don't know," I told them.

Simon smiled sadly and tightened his hold on Adam.

"Please don't dismiss me," I said, frustrated and pleading. "I've had one business taken away from me by homophobic assholes. I won't let it happen again." They stared at me now, listening. "We have to do something, because if we can't fight for this"—I waved my hand at the apartment—"if we can't fight for this"—I motioned my hand between the three of us—"then what have we got to fight for?"

They both stared at me, not blinking and not saying anything. I shook my head and sighed, the fight in me gone. "I need to take a shower," I whispered. "I smell like the kitchen."

I left them standing in the small living room. The smell of the food I'd just cooked lingered on me, and it wasn't uncommon for me to shower after working. But this time it wasn't to rid the smell of fish or grease. I wanted the heat of the water to unknot my shoulders and to wash away the feeling of unease that seemed to have settled on my skin.

I stood with my head under the streaming hot water, feeling the ache in my muscles slowly dissipate. I had no clue what the solution was, but I knew whatever we decided would be for the three of us. It wasn't ideal—it was perfect where we were—but we'd work it out together.

Feeling a little better, I got out of the shower, dried off, and wearing only a towel, walked out to find Adam and Simon were getting ready for bed. I crawled up onto my side and when Adam got into his spot, I pulled him against me. "You're warm," he murmured. "And you smell good."

I chuckled at him then lifted my head. "Sy?"

His lip curled into a half-smile and he got into bed, quickly sliding in next to Adam, wrapping him up between us like we normally did. I reached out and traced my fingers through Adam's hair and told him, "Sy's right. We'll figure something out. Won't we?"

Simon sighed. "Yeah. We sure will."

But when we woke up the next morning, Simon's side of the bed was empty.

Adam shot out of bed. "Sy?"

I followed him. He checked the bathroom. "Sy?" Then he went to the living room. "Simon?" His voice was getting higher, more anxious as he looked around the empty apartment. "*Simon?*"

Adam threw the front door open and stepped out into the hall, where Simon stood fully dressed with his phone to his ear. He looked at Adam, then looked into the apartment at me, then looked back at Adam and grinned.

Adam was as naked as the day he was born. So was I, but I wasn't standing in the hall where any of the cleaning staff could see me. Adam was. Simon grabbed his hand and pulled him into the apartment, closing the door behind him.

He'd obviously been in his office but had come when he'd heard Adam call for him. He was still mid-conversation with whoever was on the other end of the line, but he led Adam to the couch and sat him down. He pecked his lips to Adam's, then motioned me over to join Adam on the couch. He kissed my lips.

"Yes, I can bring those," he said into the phone. He had a light in his eyes, an air of excitement. "No, the three of us will be there in about an hour. Yes. Of course. Okay, see you soon."

He hung up, looked at a very naked me and Adam, and grinned. "I can't believe I'm going to say this," he started. "But you guys are gonna need to get dressed."

"Why?" Adam asked. "Sy, what are you doing?"

"Why? Because I'm sure my parents don't want to see you naked," he said with a smirk. "And *I'm* not doing anything. *We* are going to see my parents. I think I've found a way to beat Hartley."

Parents.

I was going to meet Simon's parents.

Fuck.

Adam had met them before, of course, and they both told me I had nothing to worry about. But that didn't stop me from panicking. I'd never 'met the parents' before. Not the parents of someone I was dating. I'd never been introduced as someone's boyfriend before.

"They know we're together," Simon told us in the car on the way over there. He was driving, Adam was shotgun, and I was in the back.

Ugh. I put my hand to my stomach, pushing down the sudden lump of unease in my gut.

Simon looked in the rearview mirror at me. "I told them all about you," he said, like he'd discussed the weather with them.

"Jesus." I exhaled loudly. "What did they say?"

Sy laughed. "Well, Mom was pissed off at first. I got the whole spiel about how wonderful Adam was and how I shouldn't have let him go, she thought we were in love, and Adam was the sweetest boy she'd met, blah, blah, blah."

Adam's mouth fell open. "Did she think we'd broken up?"

Simon chuckled and nodded. "And she ripped into me for it too." He shook his head. "So after I'd explained that no, we were still together, but we'd met Wil and now we were just three instead of two..." He looked at me again in the mirror and smiled.

"Anyway," he went on to say, "she was shocked, yes. But after I'd told her all about you, she was fine. She's looking forward to meeting you."

Oh. "And your dad?"

Simon shrugged. "Well, I mostly talked to him about work, but no doubt Mom told him."

And before I could say anything else, Simon pulled the car into a driveway. It was a very expensive-looking driveway that fronted a very expensive-looking house. I hadn't been paying much attention to where we'd been going. I'd been trying to get my head around meeting Simon's parents, but looking around at the surrounding houses, I could see we were in a neighborhood that spoke of money.

The houses were huge and the lawns manicured. Simon pulled the car up to the front door, grabbed his messenger bag, and got out. Adam was right behind him, and I reluctantly followed.

"You'll be fine," Simon told me as he opened the door. "They'll love you."

He just walked in. Adam took my hand and led me inside. The foyer itself was almost as big as our living room, with marble floors and a marble staircase and grand mirrors on the walls. It looked like a museum. Sy just walked in and threw his bag on a sofa like he would at our place.

"Hey, Mom?" Simon called out as he walked on through to a fancy living room that joined an open kitchen. Holy shit... the kitchen. I'd never known what a dream kitchen looked like until I walked into it. The cabinetry was white, the countertop a solid gray marble. The appliances were stainless steel and state-of-the-art with the fixtures and fittings to match.

Then a woman walked out of what appeared to be a walk-in fridge with her arms full of produce. She was slim, wearing all white, with short, spiky gray hair, and funky purple glasses. She looked oddly like Simon, and she grinned when she saw him. He quickly grabbed the eggs and a bag of mushrooms off the top of her armful of food and kissed her cheek. As she put the rest of the grocery items on the marble countertop, Simon turned to face us. He smiled when he saw Adam and I were holding hands.

"Good morning, Mrs. Stanford," Adam said with his usual grin.

"Good morning, Adam," she said with a warm smile. Then she looked at me, and I thought for a moment she could hear my heart hammering in my chest.

Simon smiled proudly. "Mom, this is Wil."

"Ma'am," I said with a nod, by way of greeting.

Mrs. Stanford said, "Simon told me all about you."

Oh.

Adam slid his arm around my waist and gave me a squeeze, but Simon changed the subject. "Mom, what's with all the food?" he asked, looking over the groceries on the counter.

"Well, you told me the three of you would be coming over," she explained. "I thought I'd cook you all a breakfast."

"Okay." Simon shrugged. "Where's Dad?"

"Upstairs. He'll be down in a moment, I'd imagine." Mrs. Stanford then looked at Simon. "So, care to tell me what this ever-so-important meeting is about?"

Simon looked at me and Adam, then back at his mother. "I asked Dad to buy our hotel."

CHAPTER SIXTEEN

"YOU WHAT?" Adam and I asked in unison.

Simon looked at us. "I asked Dad to buy the hotel," he said again. Then he looked to his mother. "It makes sense."

Mrs. Stanford put a heavy wooden chopping board on the countertop and looked at Simon. "His business isn't in hotels or even in the hospitality sector, Simon. Why would he be interested in buying your hotel?"

Simon shrugged. "Well, he's not interested." Simon picked up a raw mushroom and took a bite. "I asked him to meet with me so I can convince him."

His mother smiled. "How are your negotiation skills?"

"How are whose negotiation skills?" someone said in a deep voice behind us. When I turned to see who had spoken, there stood a man who had to be Simon's father.

He was tall, dressed in what looked like a golfing outfit, with dark, graying hair. Although they didn't look that similar—Simon was more like his mother—there was something about him that made the genetics of Simon make complete sense.

Mr. Stanford walked into the kitchen and stood beside

his wife. He stole a mushroom off the board and popped it in his mouth, just like Simon had done.

"Hey, Dad," Simon greeted him.

"Boys," his father answered.

"Hi, Mr. Stanford," Adam said cheerfully.

Then Simon introduced me. "Wil, this is my dad, Richard Stanford."

"Wilson Curtis, sir," I said and offered him my hand, which he shook.

"Ah, yes," he said with a nod. "Sylvia told me about"— he looked at the three of us—"this new arrangement."

Simon's mother collected a bowl from a cupboard. "All I told him was what Simon told me."

Oh, shit. I hoped to God they weren't going to discuss what they thought of the type of relationship their son was in right there in front of us.

Simon stood with his back to the countertop and lifted himself so he was seated on it. It was obvious he was comfortable here and in front of his parents. He was totally at ease, regardless of the fact he'd just introduced them to his two live-in boyfriends. "There's not much to tell, Mom," he said simply. "At first, there was Adam and me, and now there's Adam and me and Wil."

Mrs. Stanford looked at the three of us. "And you're all happy with that?"

Simon rolled his eyes, and Adam nodded. And I was on the verge of freaking out and needed something to do with my hands. I waved my hand toward the food on the counter. "Can I help you with anything here?"

Mr. Stanford interrupted, "You boys should come around at this time more often if it means I get cooked breakfast," he said with a grin. Then he looked at his son. "Come on, show me these reports you brought with you."

Simon looked at Adam and me. "You guys all right in here while I have a quick word with Dad?"

"Of course they are," his mother answered for us. Then she looked at me and answered my earlier question, "Of course you can help. Oh, you're a chef, yes? I'm sure that's what Simon told me."

"Yes, ma'am."

She pushed the chopping board toward me and smiled. "Then be my guest."

Simon smiled at us and followed his father, leaving Adam and me with his mom.

I smiled back at her and stepped over to the counter. "So, what's on the menu?"

"I thought we'd have omelets with ham, peppers, mushrooms, and cheese," she answered. "Does that sound all right?"

"It sure does!" Adam said, moving over to stand on the other side of Simon's mother. "Sounds great! What can I do?"

Mrs. Stanford smiled sweetly at Adam. It was obvious she liked him. "Can you make coffee, dear?"

Adam beamed. "Sure can."

While Adam rummaged through cupboards and set about making a pot of coffee, I started to deseed and slice peppers, and dice the ham and mushrooms.

And it was really very easy. Simon's mom wanted to know how chefs got their omelets so light and fluffy, so I gave her a crash course on whisking and timing. Adam made coffee and toast, and we talked and laughed a little, and after I'd called her ma'am for about the tenth time, Mrs. Stanford hummed quietly beside us. "Well, I can say one thing about Simon," she mused out loud. "He has a thing for well-mannered, polite boys."

Adam grinned proudly, and I blushed seven shades of scarlet. "I, um... I, uh..."

"Don't be nervous, dear." She patted my arm. "I'll admit I was shocked at first, when he told me, but I wasn't surprised. The fact that my Simon loves two people at the same time doesn't surprise me at all."

"It's, um..." I started and exhaled. "It's just... well, it's just that we're hardly conventional."

Mrs. Stanford smiled fondly. "My dear, there isn't much about Simon that is conventional." As she got the service trays ready, she told us, "He's never done anything the conventional way." She sighed. "You know, when he was a baby and learning to walk, he'd get cranky if anyone tried to help him. And riding his bike, he wouldn't have the training wheels." She shook her head at the memory. "Said he'd prefer to fall off and learn how to do it right the next time rather than have something propping him up."

She looked at us both. "You boys probably know all too well how stubborn he can be," she said with a fond smile. "Wouldn't go to work for his father. He flat-out refused. But as much as it drove his dad crazy, he respected him for it."

Mrs. Stanford gave us a warm smile. "So for Simon to come here asking for help, or even advice, tells me all I need to know about how he feels about you two."

I didn't quite know what to say to that. Apparently neither did Adam. He looked at me, his face a mixture of smugness, shyness, and surprise.

"Are the omelets done?" Mrs. Stanford asked, snapping me out of my daze.

"Yes, ma'am."

We plated everything up and carried breakfast to the patio where Simon and his dad were sitting in the morning sun. The reports Simon had organized for the hotel owners and their accountants were now printed off and on the table in front of them. They were discussing figures but promptly stopped and packed away the papers so we could all eat breakfast.

And it was good, too. The quiet hums of appreciation while everyone ate were an excellent indication they enjoyed it. And it wasn't until plates were empty that anyone spoke.

Simon sipped his coffee and took a deep breath before he spoke. "Dad's company is in imports and exports, but I asked if he could at least meet with the owners to talk investment."

Simon's father looked at him and sighed. "I'm not sure, to be honest, Simon. If they've met with Hartley on-site already, then they seem happy with his proposal."

Simon shook his head. "Dad, they'd be happy with anyone's money. The owners told me themselves they don't like what the man stands for."

Mr. Stanford stared at Simon, then at Adam and me for a long moment. "And this Hartley guy only wants to buy it to get rid of the gay-friendly hotels?"

Simon nodded. "Yes. He's a homophobe with the finances to back his beliefs." Then Simon looked at his mother. "You remember this Hartley guy's political campaign? He wants to get rid of us one way or another."

Simon's mother nodded. "Of course I remember."

"I'm not saying it's not true," Mr. Stanford conceded. "I just find it hard to believe someone would garner a real estate portfolio like his with such a blatant agenda."

"Yeah, well, money talks, apparently," Simon said curtly. He sat back in his chair, and I could see he was getting angry.

Mr. Stanford looked at his son. "I'm sorry, Simon. It's just business."

"No, it's not," Simon's jaw bulged and he lifted his chin proudly. "It's more than that. It's what I've worked my ass off for, over three years, getting that place just perfect. It's more than just a business or a job to me. It's my home." Simon looked at Adam, then at me. "It's *our* home."

I could tell Simon's father was an astute businessman. He needed to know what kind of commitment he'd be getting for his investment.

"Mr. Stanford?" I interrupted, trying to reinforce Simon's argument. Figuring I had nothing to lose, I offered him the money from selling my restaurant and my parents' house. I wanted him to see what it meant to me. "I have a little over five hundred thousand dollars. I know it's pennies compared to what you'd be talking for the hotel, but it's all I've got. And I'm more than prepared to offer it to you in return for our three names to be included on that contract."

Everyone at the table stared at me.

Simon's father smiled like he was dealing with a child. Maybe he was.

I cleared my throat so my voice didn't betray my nerves. "I know we'd only be talking about five percent, probably less, but it's an invested interest. If we"—I looked quickly to Adam and Simon—"have part ownership, no matter how small it is to you, it's *huge* for us, and it's an incentive for us to give it everything we've got."

"Wil," Simon whispered.

I turned to him, taking in his wide eyes. He looked a little pale. "Simon, I'm serious."

"I can see that," Mr. Stanford replied.

I saw a flicker of something in his eyes, so I struck while the iron was hot. "I think you're worried about commitment or dedication from us for your investment, and that's fair enough. But, Mr. Stanford, we're a partnership—Simon, Adam, and myself. We're not a legally-bound partnership, but we'd request it be reflected on the contract of sale for whatever percentage it works out at, and we'd expect dividend returns as such."

Mr. Stanford smiled again, but this time with what looked like an inkling of respect.

"You're confident in this"—he searched for the right word, looking between the three of us—"this *partnership*, that it would withstand the pressure of working together, living together, running a business—"

"Yes," I cut him off, answering without hesitation and without doubt. "Absolutely. It's the three of us or none of us."

Simon's father looked from me to his son. "Simon?"

Simon stared at me for a long moment and I was expecting him to speak to me, to tell me to butt the hell out, but then he looked at his father. "I can almost match Wil's offer," he said. "If I can use Grandma's trust money. That will give you at least nine hundred thousand."

His father blinked, taken aback. "You'd do that?" he asked, clearly surprised. "That's a huge commitment, Simon."

"I know it is, Dad. But that's what this is. That's what I've been trying to tell you!" Simon huffed out a sigh and ran his fingers through his hair. "Anyway, what Wil said earlier is right. It's the principle of the thing. If we let Hartley win, then we stand for nothing. We're not just trying to keep the hotel. I want to prove to that asshole we won't apologize for being gay."

I swear, in that moment, I could have thrown my arms around Simon and kissed him so fucking inappropriately in front of his parents. But instead, I grinned at him, and I realized at that point, even if we didn't get to keep the hotel, that we'd be okay. Simon wanted to stand up for who he was and for what he believed in, and right there, in front of his father, he just had.

I was so proud of him.

Mr. Stanford sat back in his chair, looked at the three of us, and sighed. Then he looked at his son but still said nothing.

"Just meet with them," Simon said, resigned, pleading. "Meet the owners, meet that Hartley prick if you want to. No promises, no obligations, just meet with them."

Mr. Stanford looked at Simon. "One meeting. No promises."

Simon clapped his hands, and in the next second was on his feet, walking off into the garden with his phone to his ear.

I was still buzzing when we got back home. Simon had organized a meeting with the owners for the following afternoon at the hotel and even told them to extend the offer to Hartley. He wore a grin from ear to ear.

"I thought your dad was going to say no," I told him. "I mean, it's a huge investment. We're talking millions of dollars, so I understand why he's so hesitant."

Simon nodded. "He takes all business negotiations seriously, and if he thought for one moment we weren't committed to this, he wouldn't even consider it."

I cupped his face in my hands and kissed him. "I'm committed to this."

He smiled and whispered, "I'm committed to this, too."

I turned to look for Adam, wondering why he wasn't in between us. He was staring at us, and he looked...wrong. It took me a moment to realize what it was that was different.

He wasn't smiling.

"Adam, what's wrong?" I asked, alarmed. "I thought you wanted this? You said before you'd love to own part of this place."

His mouth opened and closed, twice. Simon stood by my side and we waited for Adam to find the words he was looking for.

"I can't be a part of it..."

Simon frowned. "Why not?"

Adam shrugged and spoke to the floor. "I can't... I don't have that kind of money to put in..." He shrugged again.

"It doesn't matter about the money," I told him. "The money isn't important."

"Yes, it is," he answered.

"Not to me, it isn't," I replied, just as quietly.

"I've got nothing to give," he whispered.

Simon's frown deepened. "How so?"

Adam looked at him then, almost teary-eyed. "You run a business, and you"—he looked at me—"ran your own business. You're both qualified and have the finances to do this, and I don't. How can we be equal thirds when we're not equal at all?"

"I'll tell you why, Adam," I said seriously. "Because without you, we'd have nothing."

His eyes shot to mine, confused. So I walked over to him, and taking his face in my hands, I told him, I told him the exact truth, honesty laid bare. "Without you, I wouldn't be here in Florida. Without you, I wouldn't have been invited into your lives, invited into your world. Adam, it's you who holds us together. I love Simon, very much," I said, like he wasn't standing right there. "And I know he loves me, but without you, there wouldn't be an us."

Simon took Adam's hand. "Adam, look at me," he ordered gently. Only when Adam's eyes met his did he continue. "Wil's right. It's three of us or none of us. All the money in the world doesn't mean a damn thing compared to what you mean to us."

"Without you, Adam, we've got nothing," I told him again. "The things you give us can't be counted or measured. I mean it, Adam, you are everything to us."

"Thank you," he said with a sad smile. "But I just don't feel very equal."

The thought of him feeling anything but equal just tore at me. "Adam, if you want, I'll cancel the offer. We'll call Simon's dad and say we can't do it."

He looked at me with wide eyes. "What?"

"If you're not comfortable with this, then we don't do it. It's as simple as that," I told him. "We'll find something else."

Adam frowned. "I don't want to find something else. This is my home. I belong here."

"You belong with us as an equal third," Simon said. "So the offer stays?"

Adam looked at us both, then slowly, he nodded.

I lifted his chin and pressed my lips to his. "I love you, Adam Preston."

Then Simon kissed him, soft and sweet, and rested his forehead on Adam's, holding their faces together. Simon didn't have to tell him he loved him. Jesus, it was there. Without having to say a single word, it was *right* there.

And later that night, Simon and I proved to him, proved to every inch of him, just how much he meant to us. There was no way, no possible way he could have doubted us.

At four o'clock the next afternoon, the two owners arrived with a smug Hartley. Simon's father had arrived ten minutes before, along with his lawyer. They were impeccably dressed in suits I could only dream of owning. They were extremely professional, no nonsense, and there to talk business.

Hartley had been told he was meeting the owners again and another interested party, and that was all he'd been told. Needless to say, Hartley was surprised by who he met —or rather, surprised by the obvious wealth and business expertise he met—and his smug attitude got defensive from the very beginning.

No, Mr. Stanford had no experience in buying or running hotels, but to him it was just a product. A profitable product, selling for an undisclosed figure, which he could purchase and receive returns for, and *that* was a concept he understood very, very well.

Adam, Simon, and I watched from the bar. Mr. Stanford had said they would be merely discussing potential interest at this point, and multimillion-dollar decisions were best made with the head, not the heart, so he'd prefer it if we sat out.

But Simon's father had also insisted they sit at a particular table, one that was conveniently close enough for us to hear every word.

They exchanged pleasantries and got straight to business. Simon's father declared outright he was interested in the purchase of the hotel. He didn't even give Hartley time to blink. He asked a slew of questions, and I realized then there was a reason he was so successful in business.

Simon's mother was right. Her husband and her son were so alike when it came to business—the quiet seriousness, the professional confidence, how they held their stares but not their tongues.

Mr. Stanford requested his accountant be sent all necessary information, which we knew he already had—courtesy of Simon's reports—but no one else was privy to this. He needed this to look legit. He told the owners it would be his intention to leave the hotel operational, just as it was. He gave his word to them that he had no immediate plans for redevelopment and that he saw no need to overcapitalize with further development when it was already profitable as it was.

I figured there was no other reason for him to mention redevelopment except to have a shot at Hartley. He wanted to show the owners that it was about the business, not about personal vendettas against gay people.

As predicted, when the meeting was over, no actual figures had been discussed, no deals had been done. But contact had been made, and Hartley knew he wasn't the only horse in the race.

As the meeting disbanded, Simon went over to speak to the two owners while his father stood and talked to Hartley. "So, branching into the hospitality sector?" Hartley asked, though he wasn't making conversation. He was fishing for information.

"Considering it, yes," Mr. Stanford replied.

"So, you married?" Hartley asked, out of nowhere.

Mr. Stanford blinked in apparent surprise at the personal question. "Yes. My wife and I have been together for thirty years."

Hartley nodded and smiled, looking pleased. "Ah, for a moment I thought you might have been *one of those...*"

Mr. Stanford's lips curled. "One of those what?"

Hartley made no effort to hide his disgust or the volume of his voice. He nodded toward Simon and gave a pointed stare to us. "One of those filthy fags."

And I swear the world stood still.

I saw Simon turn to face him, obviously having heard what Hartley had just said, and Adam gasped beside me. But it was Mr. Stanford's reaction that surprised me the most.

He moved so quickly I barely saw it, but he was now standing right in front of Hartley, all up in his face. And he was seething. He spoke in a menacing whisper, "That *filthy fag* you're talking about is my son. So I suggest you watch your fucking mouth."

Hartley's face paled, and he tried to recover but couldn't. "That figures," he said weakly, taking a small step back.

Simon's father stared at him for a long, unnerving minute before he walked over to where Simon and the two owners were standing. He spoke to Simon first. "I'm sorry I doubted you when you told me what an ass he was."

Then he spoke to the two owners. "I'll offer you whatever he's offered. I won't offer you any more or any less, but I trust your good conscience will know which is the better deal."

Then his lawyer friend was beside him, briefcase in hand, indicating their time here was up. Mr. Stanford sighed. "I have another meeting to go to right now, but I'll have my legal team draft something up."

Hartley stalked past them, muttering something else about queers as he went.

One of the owners glared in total disbelief to what she'd just witnessed, the blatant hatred inside the man. Then she looked back at Simon's father. "Mr. Stanford, I believe we'd be very interested in discussions with you."

They exchanged some contact details, and the owners left. Mr. Stanford told us he'd be in touch. He hugged his son, told me he'd need some paperwork on my finance proposal to buy our way into this deal, then he told us he'd see us soon and left.

I looked to Simon. His eyes were wide, and a look of disbelief morphed into a grin. I imagined it matched mine.

Three weeks later, we became legitimate partners with a combined ten percent share of the hotel. Simon's father's business owned the rest. We worked together, we lived together, and we played together. The three of us. Regardless of ownership percentages, we were and would always be equal thirds.

CHAPTER SEVENTEEN

IT HAD BEEN six months since I'd officially moved here, started working at the hotel, and become a part of Adam and Simon's world. Six months.

It hadn't all been easy. There had been some adjustment issues as the three of us got used to being part of a threesome. But the few hiccups we had were minor, and the better we got to know each other, the easier it became. The work was fun, the sex was unbelievable, and the laughs were plenty. It had been without doubt the best six months of my life.

Six months.

My God, the time had flown.

It was very fitting how the Key West annual Pride celebration was the same weekend as my six-month anniversary. It was my first. It most certainly wouldn't be my last. But I was so excited.

Nowhere near as excited as Adam, but excited nonetheless.

I couldn't wait to see the festival, see the crowds and all the people who were out to celebrate who they were. Key

West was drowning in rainbow-colored everything, the hotel was booked solid, and there was a buzz on the streets. It was like a high.

Yes, we were busy. But there was no way, no way in hell, we were missing Pride. No. Fucking. Way.

The entire guest list of the hotel was going to the festivals anyway, so the fact the restaurant was closed for the evening didn't affect anyone.

The hotel was quiet, eerily so. Nearly everyone had left already. I was just doing some prep work to get a head start on tomorrow, knowing I'd probably be hung over and not too motivated. Simon was in the reception area finalizing next month's rosters or something, and Adam... well, Adam was being Adam.

He'd gone to collect some shirts for the three of us to wear so we all matched. He told anyone who'd stand still long enough that he had *two* live-in boyfriends. When we went out, he didn't have to tell anyone—it was written on his shirt.

Literally.

He'd found a shirt online, which he'd just *had to have*, and wore it to death. He wore it every time we were all together, he wore it out, and he wore it to work. People usually looked twice, and he'd just grin.

Because written on his shirt was *I'm With Them* with two hands pointing in either direction. And the fact that he was usually snuggled in between us with one arm around each of us meant we always got a few stares.

I'd certainly gone from one extreme to the other. From not being out in public with any guy to now being out in public with two. At the same time.

But I'd soon learned I had nothing to hide. Maybe back in Alabama I had, but not here.

Most of the guys at the local clubs and bars soon got used to us all being together. Having threesomes was nothing new to most of the gay men in this town, but making it a permanent thing wasn't too common.

I didn't know if they admired us, envied us or thought we were crazy. Possibly all three. But they sure liked to watch us dance.

Tuesday nights were our usual night out. Our only night out together. It was all we could ask for, really, for the three of us to be away from the hotel at one time. So we made the most of it. We went out for dinner, we had a few drinks, and we danced. Then we spent Wednesday mornings out for breakfast, usually at Dee's café.

I smiled at the memories of the last six months and finished cleaning up the kitchen prep area. I looked at my watch, wondering where Adam was so we could go to the Pride festival already. He was supposed to be back by now, and when I heard Simon's voice, I assumed it would be Adam with him.

"Wil?" Simon called. "Can you come out here for a second?"

It was a little weird that they didn't come in and see me, but when I walked out to the foyer, I realized why.

It wasn't Adam with Simon.

It was Rod.

As in my ex-whatever-you'd-call-it from Alabama.

To say I was shocked would have been an understatement. I looked around to see who he might be here with.

"I, uh, I came by myself," he said quietly. "I came to see you."

I blinked. I was at a complete loss. "Why?"

Rod glanced at Simon, who was looking back and forth between us.

"Rod, this is Simon. Anything you have to say, you can say in front of him. I'll only be telling him what you said anyway."

Rod looked seven shades of uncomfortable. "I, um, I saw you when you came back to Dalton. On Main Street, do you remember?"

I nodded. "I saw you."

"You didn't speak to me."

"I had nothing to say to you." I shook my head. "How did you even find me?" There was no way Callie would have told him.

"The real estate office gave me your forwarding address," he said with a shrug. "I told them I had official business..."

I shook my head. "Jesus Christ, Rod, what are you doing here?"

Rod looked at Simon, then back to me. "I, um... I, uh..." He was struggling to say what he wanted—it was almost painful to watch.

"Rod, just say it."

He swallowed, hard. "I want you to come back."

I couldn't help the bubble of laughter that escaped me. "You *what?*"

"I wanted to apologize," he said quietly. "And I just... I thought maybe we could talk."

I looked at him. "We're talking now."

Rod turned to look at Simon again, so very uncomfortable having to say this in front of someone else. "I miss having you—"

"Rod, stop," I said, putting my hand up. "If you're asking me to go back, back to hiding and lying, then just stop." I walked over to Simon and slid my arm around his waist. "I'm never going back. I have a life here, a life where I don't have to hide, and no one would ask me to. I'm not a dirty little secret. Not anymore."

And just then, Adam all but ran through the front doors, to where we were. He had a bag in his hand. "I got them all to match!" he cried, before he looked up to see us. He saw Simon with his arm around me, and he could no doubt feel the tension in the air. He stopped, then walked slowly around Rod over to us. "Who's this?"

"Adam, this is Rod."

I could almost see the name turning over in his head. Rod. *Rod...*

Simon whispered, "Wil's ex."

Adam spun to face Rod, and without taking his eyes off him, he stepped closer to us, and put his hand on me. It was possessive and territorial. It was fucking perfect.

Rod looked at the three of us. His brow furrowed, confused. "I thought you were with him," he said, giving a nod toward Simon.

"I am," I said. "And I'm also with Adam."

He blinked. "Both of them?"

I smiled. "Both."

Simon looked at Rod and leaned in and kissed me, right on the mouth. Then like Rod wasn't there, he asked Adam, "They had the shirts?"

Adam nodded and reached into the bag. He pulled out three blue shirts with *I'm With Them* and the two hands pointing in opposite directions on them. He threw one to each of us.

I grinned. "Perfect."

Simon took off his shirt, showing off his ripped torso and the delicious *V* that ran under his cargos. "We need to get going. We're supposed to meet at Dee's." He slipped on his new shirt, which I was sure Adam had deliberately ordered one size too small.

Ignoring Rod altogether, Simon held out his hand. "Give me your shirts and I'll run them upstairs."

He was doing this deliberately, so Rod would have to see me half-naked. I shook my head at him but took off my shirt.

The last six months here had done my body good. All that running, healthy eating, and fucking-for-exercise, as Adam called it, had me pretty trim, fit, and tanned. Rod noticed, that was for damn sure. His eyes just about fell out of his head. Simon failed to hide his smirk, took our shirts, and disappeared upstairs.

I looked at Rod, who was now looking really out of place, and smiled. "I'm sorry you wasted your time. Maybe you should have phoned first?" Considering he'd never called me, *not once*, to see if I was okay, I knew that was highly unlikely. I considered telling him he should have called me every day, he should have come to see if I was okay when the entire town had turned against me, and that he should have defended me.

He was clearly uncomfortable and a little torn. I sighed. "Look. It's not about being in the closet. Because believe me, that's something I understand well. But it's about love, even behind closed doors. The whole town didn't need to know, but you could've at least *spoken* to me. Or at least not turned your back on me when I needed you most."

He nodded sadly. There was so much I could've said. But I didn't. The truth was, I just didn't care. Not anymore. Instead, I told him, "But we're heading out now. The Pride festival is on."

"Yeah, so I found out," he mumbled with a frown.

"Did you need a lift somewhere...?" I asked, trying diplomatically to get rid of him.

"Ah, no," he whispered, shaking his head. "That's fine."

Simon came back down the stairs and waited for us at the door, so we walked out the front of the hotel, and Rod had no choice but to follow.

He started to say something again, but I stopped him. "Goodbye, Rod."

With a sad nod and shake of his head, he got into the rental car and pulled out.

Adam laughed. "What a douche." Then he shook his head at me. "I'd really like to say something about your taste in men but it would only incriminate Sy."

I snorted out a laugh. "And you don't include yourself in that?"

Adam rolled his eyes. "Oh, no, not at all. I'm perfect. Anyone can see that."

I laughed, and the three of us headed out in our matching shirts that showed the world exactly who we were with.

Like they could ever doubt us.

EPILOGUE

HOLIDAY SEASON WAS ALWAYS BUSY. Our hotel was booked solid for the summer, as it had been for the five years I'd been there. The Florida Keys was a magnet for people, gay or straight, looking for some holiday hook-ups and parties, or just a quiet recharge of soul.

This year was no different.

I was head-down, tail-up in the kitchen. It was my domain in our business, and my staff was excellent and fun to work with. I guess I'd become one of those annoying people who'd found their dream job and was lucky enough to go to work every day.

Adam was busy in his bar, as always, but he'd also included event management in his everyday duties. It was something he'd evolved into, and he loved organizing parties and seeing them through, but where he really shined was when he stood behind the bar. He'd wear his cargos, flip-flops, and a tank top, and a leather strand necklace hung snug around his neck. He got to talk and laugh with clients, telling them stories or listening to theirs, giving them a smile or an ear as needed, and they loved him. He was in his element.

Then there was Sy. He ran the entire business like a well-oiled machine. His strengths were finances and marketing strategies, and he really was the driving force behind our success.

I smiled as I remembered the way he'd laughed when he'd been between Adam and me last night.

"Hey, quit looking so happy," Sydney said, nudging me with her elbow. We were standing together at the large eight-burner gas cooktop. I was steaming fish and she was checking the crab bisque. "You're making the rest of us look miserable."

I snorted, unable to contain my grin, and never said a word. I plated up my fish, giving the final touches of perfection, and hit the bell so the waiter could take it. Without stopping, I grabbed the next order and started putting it together.

"I don't even have to guess," Sydney continued as we both worked. "There's only one reason you smile like that."

I threw a rib eye on the hot plate. "Two reasons."

She rolled her eyes. "Well, yes. But it's a two-for-one deal, so I include them as one."

"True."

We would always talk as we worked, prepping, chopping, or cooking, presenting, plating, it didn't matter. We just had this easy-talking, no-questions-asked way about us. Sure, technically she was my staff, but Sydney had become one of my closest friends. She'd been with her guy for three years now, and we vented, laughed, and cried when things got us down.

Living with two guys as a permanent threesome wasn't always roses and sunshine. And Sydney, who claimed one man was more than enough, would quite often say she had no clue how we made it work.

We just did.

The music around the bar got louder. "Someone's having a party out there," she said, nodding toward the sound. I wasn't too concerned because the dinner shift was almost over, and sometimes the parties started at breakfast.

But then the music cut, and a very familiar voice boomed over the PA system. "If I could have your attention for a moment. Wilson Curtis, you're required at the bar, please."

Adam.

"What the freakin' hell is he up to?" I mumbled. I looked at the four plates in front of me, of four different orders. The steak wasn't even done yet. "I'm not done here."

Sydney stuck her head out to have a look. She was smiling when she turned around. "You better go."

I wiped my hands on my apron and grumbled under my breath as I walked out from the kitchen, through the tables of people who were all now watching me. It was getting dark and took me a second to realize that Simon and Adam were standing in the middle of the otherwise empty dance floor, both of them smiling.

Oh, shit. I stopped walking. There was no way this was going to end well.

"Keep walking," Adam said, waving me toward them.

A few people laughed.

"Here he is!" Sy said. "The man of the hour."

"The what?" I asked, taking a few hesitant steps.

Simon didn't answer me, instead he spoke to our watching guests. "Today's a special day for us. It was five years ago, today, that this man walked into this very hotel and into our lives. I knew he was special the moment I saw him and, well, Adam just had to have him." Adam grinned and nodded, making some more people laugh, and Simon spoke with a fond smile. "What started out as a few weeks of fun became five years of... perfection."

Oh.

I took a few last steps and put my arms out, fitting both of them against me, to a round of applause from the people watching. I soon realized Dee was there and a bunch of other friends and even Simon's parents.

I pulled back from Adam and Sy. "What is this?"

"It's our anniversary party," Adam said like I was missing the obvious.

"But our anniversary isn't for ten more days," I whispered.

Simon kissed my cheek. "Five years ago today, *we* became *three*."

Oh my God, they'd organized a surprise anniversary party for me! Even though it wasn't technically our anniversary. I always counted the day I said yes to staying as our anniversary. I kissed Simon on the lips, then Adam, to more applause and even a few surprised guests who might not have clued in on our triangular version of a relationship.

"Wait!" I said. "You made me cook dinner for everyone on my anniversary party?"

Adam bit his lip and turned back to the bar. "Cue the music! And the bar's on us tonight!"

Everyone cheered and the hotel filled with music and laughter.

Simon slid his arm around me and nuzzled into my ear. "It was very last minute, sorry."

Adam suddenly had three beers in his hands and handed one to each of us. "Is there room for one more in that hug?"

"Always," Sy said.

I opened my arm out, and Adam folded himself into the crook of my arm, where he fit perfectly. Then he pulled back and wrinkled his nose. "Ew. You stink!"

"I was gutting fish earlier!" I said. "If I'd have known you two were planning a party, I would've showered first."

Adam shook his head. "Well, that just won't do." And he pulled the breast of my chef jacket, making the two rows of buttons pop, revealing a fitted black tee underneath. Adam tossed the jacket onto the bar and grinned satisfactorily. "Much better."

A few people wolf-whistled, and I turned to Simon's parents. "I'm sorry."

They only laughed, very used to Adam and his ways. Soon we were having drinks with everyone, chatting and laughing, friends and hotel guests alike. But it wasn't long until, like magnets, we were drawn back to each other. Well, I found myself three-beers-happy with one hand in Adam's back pocket, and Simon almost got to join us when he was grabbed by Dee.

Dee was an amazing woman with her afro swept up in some gravity defying type of do, her full, coral-colored lips contrasting perfectly against her cocoa skin. She was one Sy's dearest friends, the very woman who'd taken Adam in, saving him from living on the streets. She'd been a rock in their lives and, by extension, mine.

Knowing she and Simon would be talking a while, Adam fixed his arms around me, rested his head on my shoulder and he started to sway. It certainly wasn't like our normal nightclub kind of dancing, but there was music and a makeshift dance floor, and apparently Adam didn't need anything more than that. He sighed contentedly and kissed my jaw. "Happy anniversary, Wil."

"I can't believe you two did this. You know, Syd's gonna kill me for leaving her to clean up after the dinner shift. I'll have to pay her back."

He chuckled quietly, his breath warm on my neck. "We'll make it worth your while."

"You better."

He sighed again, such a happy sound. "Can you believe it's been five years?"

"It's really flown by."

"Tell me, has there ever been a moment you regretted it?"

I pulled back so I could see his eyes and so he could see the sincerity in mine. "Never."

"Not even when I used your Wüsthof knife to open some boxes of Coronas?"

I snorted. "Not even then. That was a long time ago, and you didn't know how expensive they are."

"You were kinda really mad."

"I was," I conceded. "But then I saw how sorry you were."

"You mean how scared I was you were gonna hate me."

"I could never hate you," I said, kissing his lips softly. "Ever."

What I did hate was that Adam had an ingrown fear of rejection. Still, after all these years, his family's rejection was a wound that would never heal. So I kissed him again. "These last five years have been the best of my life. You and Sy are my missing pieces."

He put his forehead to mine and closed his eyes, and we still swayed to the music.

"Do you think these two even know they're in a crowded room?" Dee said next to us.

I looked over to find Sy smiling warmly at us. There was

no malice, no jealousy, just happiness and longing. Dee saw it too. "Oh, my Lord, boy, whatcha waitin' for?" she said, pushing Sy toward us.

Adam laughed. "You can have him back later," he said, "though I cannot guarantee he'll be in the same condition."

Dee threw her hands up and mumbled something that was more laugh than words. Simon pressed himself against my back and slid his arms around my waist, and he nuzzled his nose on the nape of my neck.

All of our friends and Simon's family were so used to seeing us together, and even on the streets of the Keys, the three of us together barely even raised an eyebrow. But it was obviously new to some of our guests. Even at a hotel for gay men, some wore the look of surprise; some wore a look of envy. Some, no doubt, were trying to figure out where all the limbs and body parts went, and some were just smoldering desire. I didn't know specific statistics, but the majority of people's fantasies of having a threesome was everyday life for us.

I was the meat in the delicious sandwich of Adam and Simon, and I fucking loved it.

What I didn't want, however, was to get a hard-on in front of everyone, and in particular, Simon's parents.

I turned between them to face Sy, and kissed him softly while Adam pressed his cheek between my shoulder blades. "Thank you for doing this."

"You're more than welcome," he murmured. "I know today's not the day you consider your actual anniversary of being here because you didn't technically agree to stay until ten days from now. But it is for me. Everything changed the day you walked in here. For me at least."

"And me," I whispered against his lips.

"Me three," Adam mumbled into my back, making me and Sy laugh.

"You know I'm not a fan of surprises, though, and Sydney's probably cussin' at me right now," I told him. "But Adam's already promised to make it up to me later."

Simon's eyes sparkled. "Did he?"

"Yep," Adam said. He was now leaning his cheek against my shoulder, looking at Simon. "I'm thinking spit-roast."

Simon's eyes fluttered closed and his nostrils flared. When he opened his eyes, his pupils were blown. I knew that look—he was fighting the need to take us upstairs and fuck us both.

Adam obviously knew that look as well. "Do you think they'll notice if we disappear?" he whispered. "Or if we just tell them all to fuck off."

I laughed at that, but then I whispered so only they could hear, "Seriously, you guys are getting me hard. When did you tell them this little party is supposed to finish?"

Simon looked at his watch. "In about an hour."

"I could pull the fire alarm," Adam suggested.

Simon smiled at him, the corners of eyes crinkling perfectly. "I think we can wait one hour."

Though it wasn't one hour, it was closer to two by the time we waited for the last of our guests to leave. Some left to go clubbing, some just went home, but when we finally turned the lights off and shut the door behind us, it was almost midnight, and after working all day, we were exhausted.

Simon pulled his tie off and threw it on the sofa, and I wrapped my arms around him. Adam was quickly behind me, pressing the three of us firmly together. After a second, his hands lifted the hem of my T-shirt and skimmed under the waistband of my jeans. "I'm tired," Adam said, "but I'm not that tired. I think I might go strip off and go to bed."

"Really?" I asked breathily.

Simon's nose ran along my jaw, sending shivers down my spine.

Adam kissed the back of my neck, and said, "Then I think Wil should lay himself on top of me, maybe slip himself inside me, and then I was thinking Sy could do what you do best, Sy, and fuck Wil while he's fucking me, because really, you know how much Wil loves it when we do that."

I moaned out a laugh, and Simon smiled as he kissed me. "Is that what you want, Wil? I thought there was a mention of spit-roasting."

"I changed my mind," Adam said, the bossy bottom he was. "Plus, it's Wil's night. We do what he loves, which is to fuck while being fucked."

I shrugged. "He has a point."

I felt the loss of his warmth as Adam pulled away and walked toward the bedroom, pulling his shirt off as he went. "Two minutes, then I'm starting without you."

Sy laughed as he kissed me, though his smile faded as he slowly tasted my mouth. His fingers dug a little deeper into my back, his arms held me a little tighter. He was hard in his dress pants, and I moaned into his mouth.

"Did I say two minutes?" Adam called out from the bedroom. "I meant right the fuck now."

Sy pulled away with kiss-swollen lips. "He's so impatient."

He sure was. By the time we got to the bedroom door, Adam was on his back in the middle of the bed, his knees bent, feet flat on the mattress, and his slick fingers pressed into his ass. *Jesus.* I'd never get tired of watching him.

I toed out of my boots, stripped off my clothes, pulled off my socks, then climbed on the bed. I squirted lube onto my fingers and knelt between Adam's open thighs, then started to suck his cock as I slipped a finger into my ass.

Adam knew me well. This was my favorite position. My cock in Adam's ass and Simon's cock in mine. He'd set the tempo, effectively fucking us both. Sometimes it was hard and fast, sometimes it was slow and tender.

Tonight it was the latter.

The frantic need and scorching desire turned into making love as soon as Simon knelt behind me. Our need became a longing, a searing and slow burn. Adam lifted his legs to the sides of his chest and I released his cock from my mouth, and Sy replaced my fingers with his own. I leaned over Adam then and kissed up his stomach, his sternum, his throat, and finally tasted his mouth, which made him moan.

I rubbed my cock over his hole, the slick slide felt like heaven, then I pressed inside him. I pushed in, breaching him with every inch of my dick. We'd stopped using condoms a few years ago, and the intimacy between us had been notched up a few gears since then. There was nothing better than feeling skin on skin—whether I topped or bottomed, it was just better.

Sy knelt behind me and rubbed his long length up and down my ass while I thrust slowly in and out of Adam. He knew it drove me crazy. Adam's tight and slick warmth was luring me toward orgasm, and Simon was feeding my pleasure.

"Sy," I groaned. "Please."

He put one hand on my shoulder and used his free hand to guide his cock into me. My movements inside Adam stilled as Simon's head breached my hole.

"Fuuuuuuuck," I groaned, long and loud.

Simon slowly pushed inside me, giving me time to adjust and driving Adam insane. "Hurry, Sy."

I kissed him to shut him up, plowing my tongue into his mouth. It was a welcome distraction from the cock I was taking in my ass. But even the stretch and burn stoked the fires of passion, and I was soon rocking my hips, urging Simon to start moving.

And sure enough, as he always did, he started to thrust into me which, in turn, made me fuck Adam.

For me, there was no more perfect moment than this.

Being buried inside Adam at the same time I was being filled to the brim by Simon was when my world fell away. I could feel Adam's heartbeat pulsing around my cock, and I could feel the swell of Simon as he rocked into me. We were a complete unit like this. A closed circuit.

I leaned up off Adam the best I could, giving him room to jack his own cock. I loved watching him writhe and gasp, and I loved it even more when his gaze locked onto Simon over my shoulder, and I could see the love in Adam's eyes.

"Oh fuck, Sy. Fuck us both. Yeah, like that, harder. I want to feel you come inside him."

"Oh, fuck," I groaned. Adam's filthy mouth set fire to my blood.

"Show us how you own us both," Adam urged, pumping himself hard. Then his legs flinched, his back arched, and he tightened around me as he came. His eyes went wide and his jaw clenched as pleasure rocketed through him. Simon fucked me harder, relentlessly wringing every ounce of ecstasy from Adam's orgasm through me, until finally I couldn't hold it back any longer.

I thrust up and into Adam, making him groan even louder, and came deep inside him. My orgasm seemed to rip from my toes, detonating pleasure like a nuclear fallout.

Every cell in my body screamed in pleasure, and I fell, spent, over Adam, still inside him, unable to move.

Then Simon chuckled into my back and kissed my spine. His body was still twitching as aftershocks racked through him. He must have come at the same time as me, and I'd missed it. "I think I blacked out there or something," I mumbled.

Adam chuckled underneath me. "That was so fucking hot."

Simon slowly pulled out of me, and I hummed, knowing he'd come inside me. I then pulled out of Adam, and the three of us collapsed on the bed, Adam in the middle, as always. He snuggled his face into Sy's chest and wrapped his arms around him. I spooned him with my arm resting heavy over the both of them, while we caught our breaths.

"You were right about what I needed tonight," I said to Adam, giving him a kiss on the back of his head.

"I'm always right," he replied.

"Hmm. Well, not always," Sy added. "You said I own you both, but I'm pretty sure the opposite is true—it's you two who own me."

Adam gave him a squeeze. "Same goes for me."

I was so spent I couldn't even open my eyes, but I smiled. "Me too."

"Always," Simon murmured.

"Always," Adam mumbled, already almost asleep.

There was never any doubt. *Always*.

The End

ABOUT THE AUTHOR

N.R. Walker is an Australian author, who loves her genre of gay romance.
She loves writing and spends far too much time doing it, but wouldn't have it any other way.

She is many things: a mother, a wife, a sister, a writer. She has pretty, pretty boys who live in her head, who don't let her sleep at night unless she gives them life with words.

She likes it when they do dirty, dirty things... but likes it even more when they fall in love.

She used to think having people in her head talking to her was weird, until one day she happened across other writers who told her it was normal.

She's been writing ever since...

Free Reads:

Sixty Five Hours

Learning to Feel

His Grandfather's Watch (And The Story of Billy and Hale)

The Twelfth of Never (Blind Faith 3.5)

Twelve Days of Christmas (Sixty Five Hours Christmas)

Best of Both Worlds

Translated Titles:

Fiducia Cieca (Italian translation of Blind Faith)

Attraverso Questi Occhi (Italian translation of Through These Eyes)

Preso alla Sprovvista (Italian translation of Blindside)

Il giorno del Mai (Italian translation of Blind Faith 3.5)

Cuore di Terra Rossa (Italian translation of Red Dirt Heart)

Cuore di Terra Rossa 2 (Italian translation of Red Dirt Heart 2)

Cuore di Terra Rossa 3 (Italian translation of Red Dirt Heart 3)

Cuore di Terra Rossa 4 (Italian translation of Red Dirt Heart 4)

Confiance Aveugle (French translation of Blind Faith)

A travers ces yeux: Confiance Aveugle 2 (French translation of Through These Eyes)

Aveugle: Confiance Aveugle 3 (French translation of Blindside)

À Jamais (French translation of Blind Faith 3.5)

Cronin's Key (French translation)

Cronin's Key II (French translation)

Au Coeur de Sutton Station (French translation of Red Dirt Heart)

Partir ou rester (French translation of Red Dirt Heart 2)

Faire Face (French translation of Red Dirt Heart 3)

Trouver sa Place (French translation of Red Dirt Heart 4)

Rote Erde (German translation of Red Dirt Heart)

Rote Erde 2 (German translation of Red Dirt Heart 2)

Printed in April 2022
by Rotomail Italia S.p.A., Vignate (MI) - Italy